Sailing Away

Sailing Away

Short Stories

by

Richard Morgan

LOST HORSE PRESS
Spokane, Washington
2000

First Edition

Front Cover Photograph by *Megan Dillon*
Author Photograph by *Elizabeth Atly*
Design by *Christine Holbert*

Library of Congress Cataloging-In-Publication Data
Sailing away: short stories/ by Richard Morgan.—1st edition
p. cm.
The leaving game—The song stealers—Killer swimming—
Viewpoint—The queen of acrofad—Absent without leave—
Manifest destiny—Gunner's mates
ISBN 0-9668612-4-8 (PAPER)
1. United States—Social life and customs—20th century—
Fiction. 2. Sailing—Fiction. I. Title.
PS3563.O87146 S26 2000
813'.6—dc21

ACKNOWLEDGMENTS

Some of the stories in this collection originally appeared in the
following journals:

"Absent Without Leave": *Zen Hornet*
"Viewpoint": *The Portland Review*
"The Song Stealers": *Colorado Review*
"The Queen of Acrofad": *Clinton Street Quarterly & Three Sisters*
"Gunner's Mates" (under the title "The Gunrunners"): *The Jetty: An
Anthology of Northwest Writers* (Clatsop Community College, Astoria,
Oregon)

The author wishes to thank the National Endowment for the
Arts for the Fellowship granted in 1982, which supplied me with
the motivation to continue writing, and without which this book
would not have come to fruition.

CONTENTS

The Leaving Game   1

The Song Stealers   27

Killer Swimming   45

The Queen of Acrofad   75

Viewpoint   89

Absent Without Leave   101

Manifest Destiny   109

Gunner's Mates   121

THE LEAVING GAME

MILLARD MACLEAN REMARKED to himself that the sky was perfect as he climbed out of his camper. The first morning light revealed the undersides of flat dark cumulus clouds growing together like an upside-down bombing pattern. Beyond the western breakwater he could see the edge of nimbus clouds, dark as the pilings along the docks, drifting in from their birth over the eastern edge of the Pacific. The morning would be cold and wet and rough. Perhaps gusty. His twenty-three foot *Bayliner* would pitch like a cork. He would be uneasy, then he would be sick over the stern. He smiled; so would everybody else, from Tillamook to Westport. Sick, groggy, slow at the helm. All the better.

He picked up his duffel from the back of the truck and walked down the ramp to his boat. The water around the hull of the *Judith-M* was the color of moss. Thick, and with a hint of predation. He pulled back the canvas cover; everything was in order. Boat cushions stowed forward in the small cutty-cabin, extra gas can in the stern by the engine box. Salmon pole secured by the helm. Radio on the dashboard. He slid his key into the ignition and left it off, then tuned in the radio to 62.5 megacycles. A voice droned, "Cape Blanco, overcast, wind from the west-south-west at eight knots, visibility eight miles. Newport, overcast . . ." He let the voice trail off into his subconscious. There were special chores to be done. He uncovered the engine—a Volvo marine inboard, clean and quiet.

Now it begins, he thought. He loosened the carburetor gas line one turn, then tightened it again. Then he pared the insulation from a wire near the starter motor. He quickly fastened a small steel box to the bared wire and then to the battery as the voice from the radio said, "Columbia Bar, overcast, wind from the southwest at fifteen knots, visibility five miles. Swells, six feet from the northwest with seas to four feet from the southwest. Small craft advisories are not in effect, but caution is advised. Cape Disappointment, overcast . . ."

Ready. He sat back into the helmseat and lit a cigarette. After a few puffs, he took a small black plastic box from his duffel and extended a tiny antenna from its top. He turned the engine ignition key to the on position and pressed the button on the box in his hand. There was a bright spark near the starter motor as the engine kicked over. He retracted the antenna and put the box into his pocket, then turned the key. The engine started without a spark. He let the engine warm up as he replaced its cover, then finished his cigarette. Just a normal Saturday down in Ilwaco, the closest harbor to the most treacherous bar on the western seaboard—the carnivorous mouth of the Columbia River. A challenge even to freighters on a calm day. And it was not quite a calm day. "I accept," he said to himself, and picked up his salmon pole to inspect the rigging.

Millard began to notice he was not only not alone, but not particularly early. The *Judith-M* rolled gently against her fenders as the wake of departing trawlers passed beneath the docks. Almost all the boats, the trawlers, the crab-pot boats and the sport boats, had either their engines running, or had some dark-coated form aboard tightening one line or another. The salmon season was so short anymore that most everyone would be out, he thought.

The *Judith-M* lurched against the rhythm of the wake swells, and a voice said, "So you're here already." It was James.

"Morning, James," Millard said, looking up from his pole at his friend. James was shorter than him, but the loose hunting jacket and the windbreaker he wore did not disguise his muscular build. James was a couple of years older than Millard; perhaps that was why he appeared more troubled, uncertain. James was staring into each passing trawler as though it were the Coast Guard and he a smuggler. He readjusted his windbreaker, then combed his hair, swallowing several times. "Morning, Mac," he mumbled.

"James, I wish you'd settle down. Here, have a smoke. The salmon won't care if your hair is messy."

"You know I don't smoke, Mac. And you know goddam well you aren't here for salmon—or have you changed your mind again?"

"Nope," Millard said. "but I really would like to hook into a gigantic Chinook . . ."

"You're the most goddam impossible man I ever met," James said. "I don't like what you're doing one bit. I only agreed to help because we've been friends for a long time. But I still don't know about this. Judith will be badly hurt, you know."

"You agreed to help because you have a thing with Judith, who is about to become an eligible widow. And because you are a frustrated old adventurer yourself, deep down under that nervous skin of yours. And you know that Judith will only be hurt for the minimum proper time. Now, sit down and have a cigarette, or I'll shove it up your nose."

"I'll break your goddam arm, Mac," James smiled, showing teeth.

"You clean livers have no sense of the thrill of risk," Millard said.

"Oh, all right, give me one. Now, what do I do?"

"Well first, you put a match to the end without the filter . . ."

"I mean later, outside!"

"Okay. We stay on channel 23 on the CB. We'll both monitor the Coast Guard on the ship-to-shore. When we hit our farthest north point and the Guard is at the southernmost swing of their patrol, I'll signal by saying 'North Jetty.' Then you come alongside and pick me up."

"That's it? That's all I do?"

"That's it. I'll handle everything else. The *Judith-M's* bilge will be full of gasoline from a loose gas line. Once we are away, I'll radio in a distress call, then start the engine by remote transmission. By the time the Coast Guard arrives, the *Judith-M* will be just a few pieces of burning debris, and I will be presumed drowned. And you, aboard the *Escapade,* will be just arriving and offer to help with the search for me. And I will be in your forward cabin taking a nap."

"You're a goddam criminal, Mac."

"Not exactly. A crook does things for gain. I'm losing a hundred grand in insurance, a house instantly paid for, two cars, a profession, and a wife who agrees she's too good for me. I like to think of this as a very altruistic gesture . . ."

"I admire your thoroughness, Mac. And your insane way of looking at things, sometimes. But for all of that, you'll still have to live with yourself."

"Well, we all have to do that, don't we, James?"

"I don't know what you're getting at."

"If you don't know by now, you never will. All you have to understand right now is a certain radio message."

"North Jetty?"

"North Jetty. Now, take this duffel bag with you aboard the *Escapade*. It's got all I'll need in the hereafter."

James gazed at him for a moment, focusing all the righteousness of his thirty-six years on a spot between Millard's eyes. Millard mentally calculated which lure would be best at the end of his line, settling on a Hoochie Squid while returning James' stare with a vacant smile. James closed his eyes and shook his head, muttering something like "get the hell going," then stepped to the dock with the duffel.

The engine of the *Judith-M* was warm and idling just below Millard's consciousness of it. He whistled a verse of "What Shall We Do with the Drunken Sailor?" as he cast off the stern line. The nimbus had grown to cover half the horizon, and far up into the sky. The saltwater of the channel was black with flecks of green; fecund.

It was a game to Millard; act easy, relaxed, this late August morning in his office at Construction Designs, Incorporated. Swivel around in his chair from his desk to the second story window and back to the desk again, chipping away at his usual pre-concentration rituals. Sharpen pencils, play leapfrog with his eraser and ruler, wad a few papers into basketballs. Act natural, full of quick shop jokes, and aspirations for the Monday following. Even a bit of sarcasm, maybe a quiet flirt with Joy, the receptionist, would help substantiate his normally blithe character—if he could muster it. The actions with which he completed this day could vary as his whim dictated, but his appearances, his attitudes must be precise. It was surprisingly difficult to play the part of one's self spontaneously; so much of his personality seemed only an unconscious miming of that which people expected of him. To Joy, he was a forty-two year old perpetual jock, fallen into indolence and professional cynicism, a mediocre architect with tendencies toward social clumsiness and manic-depressive absentmindedness. A flirtatious, married nonentity. To his senior partners, he was a marginally fair architect with occasional though not dependably frequent strokes of genius, and rather antisocial in his personal habits. A man who would rather run off for a workout at the gym than share a martini with a client. And to Judy, who preferred to be called Judith, his beloved and espoused, ah, yes. He was to her only a veneer, a rather fragile vanity, a perpetual need for placation, a crude, angular periphery she had not yet managed to polish. And also the source of her creative solvency. How much of this was his predilection, how much a defense against her adept command of his friends, his possessions, his brain? She had erupted overnight into his garden like a florid mushroom, to dazzle and alter him, to provide a measure by which he would incessantly fall short.

Amazing how clearly he saw the edges of his life—or was this too only illusion, a euphoria such as divers experience when they descend too far? But it made little difference anymore. Millard Maclean had decided to live his last full day on earth not particularly caring whether he lived up to anyone else's specifications for Millard Maclean. It was important, however, that no one suspect he had made that decision, even though it completely changed his awareness of each last, rich moment. . . .

Millard steadied himself by standing against the helm seat. The tip of the Ilwaco breakwater was just ahead; as soon as he passed it, he would be unprotected from the swells that rolled into the Columbia Bar from the Pacific. Already he could see huge combers pounding the South Jetty across the bar; at a distance of nearly four miles, he could see the wind catch the breaking swells, and white spume dancing along their crests toward the rocks. He made a quick

The Leaving Game

check for loose gear in the cockpit of the *Judith-M,* then swung the bow wide around the tip of the breakwater. He set a course down the center of the bar channel. The tide had begun to ebb; swells coming in from the sea met over the bar with the surge of the Columbia current, forming steep towers of green water several feet higher than the *Judith-M.* Millard steered the bow into the first swell and rose up over the crest, where he could see the channel buoys, the dark cliff of Cape Disappointment on the north shore, and far in the distance, the diminishing dark lines of the Columbia Bar jetties, arcing together like the pincers of a crab. Then the *Judith-M* slid down the back of the swell, and his world disappeared into a crevasse of green. On the next crest he looked astern for James and the *Escapade,* but could not find him before he slid down into the next trough. He turned on the CB radio and flipped it to channel 14. A voice said, "Breaker, breaker, *Ann-B* to *Misty Lady.* School is in at red-two, over." Millard knew there probably would be no fish around the number-two channel buoy. Someone was trying to lure the sport boats away from some hot fishing area with a transparent code. He smiled. He would head for the North Jetty as soon as he cleared the rough water of the bar. He turned to channel 23. A voice was saying, "Calling the *Judith-M,* do you read, over."

He picked up the mike. "This is the *Judith-M,* and I can read and write very well, thank you." There was a pause, then James's voice. "Mac, where are you?"

Millard pressed the button. "Beats me, but it sure is nasty out here."

"Mac, I'm just about to clear the Ilwaco Jetty. How is the bar? Over."

"I'm passing buoy seven," Millard said, "and you'd better batten down everything you can. Call me later, James. I'm busy trying not to kill myself, over."

James's voice answered. "How ironic of you. *Escapade* clear."

Millard frowned as he hung up the mike. James was trustworthy, if pressed, but he was not a good gamesman at all. No sense of humor.

The bow of the *Judith-M* veered hard to one side and Millard swung the helm to correct it. The boat slowed its broach, then broke free and righted itself on the crest of the swell. Millard realized his hands were white from gripping the wheel, and he was sweating. No time for reflection. Just time to concentrate on the angle of the bow into the swells. He breathed in deeply and exhaled, instantly wishing he hadn't. The deep breath made him realize his stomach was gurgling. Three more buoys to pass yet before the water would flatten out. He didn't dare get sick. Millard wedged himself into the space between the helm seat and the bulkhead and prepared to battle out the rollers one after another.

Millard leaned back in his swivel desk chair, and the papers vanished. He closed his eyes. Images formed, faded without time to focus on them. A fleeting pleasantness—an orange grove in the sun, a black-hulled schooner tacking across an emerald shoal, monkeys swinging, scolding, throwing half-eaten papayas. Wild ginseng glowing like devil fire in the twilight. Joy, rouging her cheeks with two fingers. College classes, thesis due, lying beneath the tall campus elm trees in pure contemptuous bliss. He turned and gazed out his second story window at the shopping mall parking lot across the street. There was a tall maple tree bricked in among the cars. The highest limbs, above him in the bright sky, revealed the first paling of autumn leaves, as if in offering. Below the limbs, young women passed, dressed in tweeds and vinyl jackets still holding the imprints of last winter's coat hangers between the shoulder blades. He wondered what compulsions drew them to the mall the moment the doors unlocked. A sale on suntan lotion? Tennis balls? This week's best seller? Spermicidal jelly? What single item would give this glaring Friday a meaning? A new body—a young and supple torso that perspired sweetness, and pungent sexual odors? Foolish; he'd just abuse it, probably worse than he took care with the old one. A young shopper, caught unaware in her sleeveless jersey? She would probably scream and slash at his face with diamond rings as he stuffed her into his shopping cart. Nothing presented itself as appropriately motivational, except perhaps a large galvanized garbage pail—one which would hold all the folders, references, projects, social contacts, and identification cards so unimportant to him beside the beauty of the golden maple leaves showing beneath the pulled-up venetian blinds. The images faded, stopped.

Millard Maclean. Architectural engineer. He was automatically thinking about it again, as he had for the past few days, weeks. Forty-two years old. Tall, thin, with a slight hook at the shoulders from years of self-consciousness about being tall and thin. A sedentary worker with but a hint of muscle tone for all his workouts at the YMCA gym. A bank account in the low five figures allowed a convenient imprecision about monetary matters. A two-story Dutch Colonial in the west hills, a view of the sunrise over the Columbia Gorge and the Cascade Range from his breakfast nook. A wife who was, although settled about the hips, still able to project an eye-catching beauty after a few hours of touch up work. The owner of a Coupe DeVille. The envy of the less fortunate anonymous. Not at all the stuff of depression, let alone termination.

In memoriam: Maclean, Millard, 42, second vice-president of Construction Designs, Incorporated, central office, Portland, Oregon, Zip Code 97214. Survivors: one Judith DeCamp, daughter of Glen DeCamp, of DeCamp and DeCamp, Legal Representatives . . .

A cathedral sanctuary formed in his mind, and several older people in black tuxedoes. A minister in purple silk with black stripes. Catholic, perhaps. Or Episcopalian. The DeCamp orthodoxy was never clear to him. He waited, in beltless white with black lapels. Judith, one-stepping down the aisle, intent on the slow wedding dirge, like a heron stalking minnows. The sprinkle of holy water caught him squarely in the left eye.

Engineering degree from Oregon State University . . . He tried to picture the campus again, couldn't except for the tall elms by the library. Honorable discharge, United States Navy . . . He vaguely remembered the ubiquitous haze-grey of the decks, the bulkheads, the foul sweat of bodies below decks on tropic nights. The pungent stench of Hong Kong streets, burnt monkey meat, raw squid, Taoist incense. The blue, smoky intonation of accented voices: "Hey, Sailor?" "Yes," he answered. He should have then; he would have, now. The smoke rose, dissipated into the autumn sunlight.

Millard Maclean. Fisherman, hunter, reader of both newspapers . . . One police officer was injured today, he had read this morning, when a middle-aged woman drove her car through the front wall of precinct headquarters, fifty yards off Seventh Avenue . . . He could understand that. The hunter instinct stirred from dormancy by a parking ticket beside a broken meter . . . How many times had he cleaned and loaded his Winchester Model 94 with no thought of deer— but that was foolish. Once, not a year ago, he had even placed the barrel under his chin against his Adam's apple and contemplated pushing the cocked trigger with his toe. Visions of his own funeral, mourners fading into Sunday brunch, discussing "that bizarre Maclean" over baked chicken breasts. It had humored him to think of himself that moment as a discarded novel. Judith losing weight in the hopes of snaring another catch, James perhaps, with her supple, reupholstered body and instantly matured insurance premiums. God knows that charming effort to please Millard was dead as long as he was locked into her still breathing.

Either way, Judith would continue to be the winner, he the payoff.

That moment of cold steel had nurtured two reflections. First, the idea of continuing to dull pencils and blotch paper with speculator's desecrations of the future in order to perpetuate the status quo of indebtedness and endless yardwork became, for the first time, completely unpalatable. Second, he realized he was enjoying that moment of pity and self-doubt, and wasn't at all certain a brain could practice those indulgences with a gaping hole in it. The trouble with suicide, he had reflected, was that one was not allowed to survive the adventure and take advantage of the change in lifestyle made possible by it. That thought had clung to him like wet cotton for weeks, culminating in a first few timid actions: a letter, an inquiry, requests for additional information . . .

There were reasons enough, though entirely personal—even whimsical, if the hours, the days of reflection and decision were discounted. But most of all, Millard Maclean was living his last official day on earth simply because he was tired of being Millard Maclean. Who was this person who kept coming to this office, who sat at this old desk, inscribing these grand, pretentious lines? He could remember the challenge of a proposed dream, the satisfaction of a first workup, the light at the end of a client's tunnel vision—but it was gone now. Each new creation supplanted some former piece de resistance, torn down to rubble in subjugation to the collective urban whim. It was as much a destructive cycle as a creative one. The only compensation was the torrential exchange of currency created by the metamorphosis of the old into the new. Jobs and money. Necessary, but completely impersonal. The metaphors, the symbols his art had supplied him had become barren, and he had stopped using them to explain life's endless phenomena to himself. But he had found no replacements, and his life had become an enigma.

Millard guided the *Judith-M* around the last black buoy to his starboard side. The swells began to flatten out as he left the path of the channel astern. He could see the gray horizon of the Pacific on three sides of him, and the swells obscured his vision only occasionally now. That was just as well. If he could keep his eyes focused on the horizon and allow his ankles and knees to absorb the yaw and pitch, he felt he had a chance of not becoming sick. He set a course due north, toward the farthest point of land he could see. Perhaps about fifteen minutes north would be the magic spot. Perhaps ten minutes. Or seventeen minutes. Millard settled for twelve-and-a-half minutes at 350 degrees true, and wished to hell that he hadn't had bacon and eggs for breakfast. He had forgotten some of the basics about small boats on large oceans, and how greasy foods tend to cling to the bottom of the stomach like wet socks. He should have had toast. James probably had toast. James was more at ease with his own frailties, and was consequently caught off guard by them less frequently. Millard hated him for that.

Millard switched on the fathometer and examined the blips of light. He calculated that ten fathoms would be the perfect depth to fish. Or maybe fifteen. Millard had just settled on twelve when he felt his forehead bead with sweat. He cursed aloud to himself for eating bacon and eggs, for cruising outside the bar on a rough day, and for taking his eyes off the horizon. He tied the helm straight with a piece of bungee and hurried to the stern. The bacon was still recognizable on the way out. He immediately felt much better, and wondered whether there were any species of fish that preferred that particular kind of jetsam. He mentally made a note to heave into a bowl next time and then soak his lures in it. One never knew. He also made a note to watch the horizon as much as possible, and to kiss the dock when he returned. He slowed the engine and unfastened his salmon pole; what the hell, one place was as good as another to pretend you're fishing. Still, Millard imagined the quick arc of the pole-tip, the singing of the star-drag. Condemned men got a last smoke, didn't they? The thought of a strike by a big Chinook all but shut down the reasonable side of his brain, what was left of it. He greased up his hands with scent killer and reached for the lure he had chosen with James's concentrated help. . . .

"I've some plans research to do downtown," Millard heard himself say to Joy. He almost laughed, tightened down his brow instead. Lying was amusing if one got really good at it. He lied for the practice, to keep in shape. The best practice was when Joy caught him in some inconsistency—a double appointment, a wrong name. The spontaneous improvisation of subsequent untruths then posed a worthy challenge. The trouble was, the lies accumulated, became difficult to remember, oppressive. Sometimes one just had to start over.

The fresh air was cooler than it appeared from behind windows. He walked slowly along Tenth Avenue, watching the first of the leaves fall from the sidewalk maples. One or two spiralled into the street corridor, tacking through the gusts of passing trucks. One yellow leaf settled onto the window of a Monte Carlo, instantly sliced into tatters by a single sweep of a wiper blade.

He stopped at the wide marble steps of the county library and sat on the stone railing. A pleasant, shaded spot for watching people and observing each movement, garment, gesture—speculating about the inner sanctum of each human puzzle. A woman marched by with high wooden heels, clacking rapidly. Pant suit. Two tiers of ceramic beads. Razor-cut shag in monochromatic strawberry blonde. Knit shawl. She was thirty-two, he thought, and worked as a clerk in either a musical instrument store or a record store.

Divorced, has one child, is out on her coffee break, rushing to buy a pint at the liquor store down the street for this evening's date with her dentist lover. . . . A young man with a day pack on his shoulder right-angled into the marble steps, up toward the library entrance. Brown bush jeans. Pullover polo shirt. Army surplus jacket. White-and-blue Nikes. Too obviously a student. Too calculated, uniform-like. Long wavy hair and wire glasses. Obviously he's a cop, undercover, on his way to check some obscure statute repealed in 1960, or hot on the trail of some notorious booknapper. . . .

"Got a cigarette?" a voice asked. Millard turned to face an unshaven figure, gaunt, but younger than he, wearing an old gray sweater, blue stocking cap.

"Don't smoke," Millard lied. He had actually cut down lately, so the untruth came easily.

"Listen, neighbor. I haven't eaten since yesterday. I'm not used to this panhandling gig. . . ." Millard suspected the touch of an expert. "I just need a couple of bucks for some food. I ain't no wino."

"Why did you pick me?" Millard practiced looking him straight in the eye. The man never faltered, gazing directly back, even lifting his brow in mock fright. Millard admired that touch.

"Because what's a dollar to you? You look like you're doing all right. But me, I got nothing." The gaunt face was warming up to it. Millard knew that a few more exchanges and he would be obligated to fork out, in payment for the man's time, the superb acting.

"What are you really going to buy with your two bucks?" Millard accused.

The man straightened. "I'm having some trouble temporarily, sir. Don't judge me by present appearances." The light went out; the man had played his best line, and looked away. It was the stroke of a master.

"I've got no money," Millard lied. "Why do you think I'm sitting here in the middle of the morning?" The man began to stroll away, wasting no more words. "Wait!" Millard shouted, waving a twenty dollar bill. "Answer my question."

The man turned only from the waist. "I don't know, buddy. Maybe you're the doorman. Maybe you're president of the sidewalk, here. Maybe you're taking a shit. Who the hell cares?"

"Indeed," Millard said, opening his hand. The money disappeared into a torn pocket. The man gave him a hard look close up to his face, then walked off in the same direction as the wooden-heeled lady. Millard cherished that last look: pure contempt.

Others passed by: an old scarfed man, a young business suit with matching vest, a girl in faded jeans with a tear across the butt. No one looked at him, or at each other, or the leaves falling from the trees. Only at the wait-and-walk sign at the corner. When the sign changed, everyone stepped in unison, like the flux of a tide. He felt moored, abandoned. Nothing to do but swing the hull into the weather, and age.

It would take little practice to become attentive when someone asked for, say, Samuel, or David. After all, he had never really gotten used to the name Millard. It would be more difficult to adjust to the age. The driver's license he had fraudulently acquired indicated he was thirty-two. He could have chosen any age; why thirty-two? He would appear old for his age. Wizened. Experienced. Perhaps more desirable than a cherubic forty-six, or a totally immature fifty-one. Perhaps some idiosyncracy that only real thirty-two year olds knew about would trip him up. Or maybe something only forty-two year olds didn't know. He smiled. Security, he knew, was insured by the prevalence of that attitude demonstrated by the hungry man: "Who the hell cares?" It would be easy to forge a bogus identity—simply become unobtrusive. He shivered.

He realized, sitting in the morning shade, that he was numb with cold. He stood, wondered which way to walk. He decided on north, because it was downhill. Immediately, he turned and walked south.

On the sidewalk at Broadway, Millard turned to drift past the shop windows under the marquees. He gazed at leather coats, silver broaches, a poster for a movie—the gunman-with-no-name. The figure rose out of the cardboard, Colt Peacemaker in his hand, saddle blanket thrown over his shoulder. Italian winos toppled from cowtown rooftops, gripping their chests. A voluptuous urchin groveled at his boots, rags slipping from her shoulders. Bullets whined through her hair, killing corrupt deputies, assassins, horses, wicker chairs. Blood trickled down his cheek. His pale steel eyes said clearly, "Fuck you, hombre."

David would need boots like that. Millard let his mouth tighten, his eyes squint. A lightning fast draw, forefinger blazing, he decided not to kill. They would be buddies instead. "Fuck you too, hombre," he answered warmly.

It would be perfect; no more V-8 cocktails for the man-with-no-name. He started north for the Jazz De Opus tavern; James would be there.

Millard was almost comfortable in the helmseat of the *Judith-M* when James's voice sounded on the radio. He decided not to answer right away; he finished his can of V-8, punched holes in the bottom and pitched it over the side. The sun broke free of the clouds for a moment, and he could feel it on the back of his neck. Then clouds darkened the sky again.

"Where are you, Mac? Over."

Millard belched, checked his pole. The line hummed taut in the breeze.

"Calling the *Judith-M*. Do you read me, Mac?"

Millard picked up the mike. "Yes, I read you, James. Did I ever tell you I hated the name 'Mac?' Over."

"Where are you, ah, *Judith-M?*"

"North Head bears one-twenty degrees at four miles. Over."

"I'll be there in about ten minutes. It's time to get ready. Over."

Millard couldn't think of an answer, so he replaced the mike in its holder. Go ahead, James. Get excited and tell the whole world what we're up to. Millard closed his eyes and rubbed them. But he supposed James was right. A month of planning had led to this moment at sea. The time of decision had come and passed. A rush of thoughts passed, but none of them were new, or different. In the afternoon, Judith would cry. In the evening, James would comfort her, along with her father, her mother, and his house. And by morning, Millard would be someone else, arriving young, green, and poor in the heartbeat of Guadelajara. He would call himself David and drink only vino blanco, gracias. After that, no one could know; planning stopped on the threshold of infinite possibility.

Millard removed the engine compartment cover and killed the engine. He loosened the gas line and then emptied his three gallon gas can into the bilge. James was waiting.

"*Judith-M* to *Escapade.* Over."

"Go ahead, Mac."

"*Escapade*, the *Judith-M* is just north of the North Jetty. North of the North Jetty. Do you read?"

"Gotcha, Mac. I'm ready."

James was such a cretin, Millard thought. He picked up his pole, began to reel in, then changed his mind. Better to appear as though he were diligently fishing when his short and perfect life came to a tragic . . . His pole arched once, twice, until the tip touched the water. Millard tightened his grip and jerked back on the handle automatically. The star drag on his reel sang as the dry line shot out. He began to reel in, just in case there was any slack in the line, but the pole bent and jerked like a dowser's wand. Feels like a salmon, he thought. Well, Hallelujah; better too late than not at all. . . .

The dark inside Jazz De Opus was lit only by glass-ball candles on the center of each wooden table. Millard ordered a Green Hungarian and sat at a table in the corner where he could view both the bar and the door. The man-with-no-name would have done that. Wild Bill should have. Millard tried to lean his chair back but it was a low vinyl couch and didn't even slide. A girl in black jeans had just brought his change when James sat down opposite him.

"You're always easy to find in a tavern, buddy," James said. "I just have to check the corners."

"Well, I feel like my back's been to the wall for years. I might as well come out of the closet," Millard said.

"Most people feel that way. I feel that way myself, sometimes. There's job pressure, there's taxes, there's traffic, there's midriff bulge, there's, there's . . ."

"Judith," Millard said. James looked away, pretended to attract the attention of the black-jeaned girl. "And there's me," Millard added.

"Yeah, there's you, Mac. But I've known you a lot longer than I've known Judith. Jesus, clear back to our high school days. You were weird even then."

"I would have said 'free spirited.'"

"Free spirited in a bug's eye. You were wound up tight as a tin foil hen. You used to walk to school because you didn't trust the bus driver. You used to write snide letters to the school paper about the women gym teachers. You used to wear gloves to the sock hops because you were afraid your palms would sweat. I used to watch you sit next to Mary

Beth at lunch and dissect your spaghetti with tweezers until she ran away. That's not free spirited; that's weird."

"I don't remember any of that. I do remember you trying out for the football team and not making first string. I remember you pushing the tight-end down the stairwell so you could take his place while he was in a cast all season. Made it look like an accident, too."

"It was an accident."

"In your proverbial bug's eye."

James leaned forward on his elbows, the grinning conspirator. "Remember the tree fort?"

"Yes. I loved that old fort." Millard leaned back. "Fairly high off the ground, as I recall. But I was shorter then."

"I don't remember whose idea it was to build it in a fir tree. We could have fallen and killed ourselves."

"That's what made it fun." Millard smiled, sipped at his Green Hungarian.

"Do you remember that trash can full of sex magazines we found in the park?"

"Oh, yes. Bad stuff in there. What ever happened to them?"

"We burned them," James said.

"But we looked through them first, didn't we?"

"We read every one of them. Then, if I remember right, we hauled them back up into the park, burned them, and then pissed on the fire."

"Worst overdose I ever had on sex," Millard chuckled. "It's amazing, Jimmy, the things we did back then."

"Why did we do those things?" James asked.

Millard raised his eyes, set his wine glass down firmly on the low wood table. "We did them because the possibility of doing them burned rich in our hot young brains. The real question, Jimmy, is why did we stop doing them?"

"We're older now, Mac. We know better."

"Better than what?"

"Better than to hurt people. Or ourselves. We're more careful."

"That's what happened to Jimmy. He became James."

"It happens to all of us, Mac. It's happening to you, too."

"No, it isn't."

"Look at you, sweating and worrying about it. We're older, slower. More brittle. You can't go back to your high school days except by remembering."

"I don't want to go back. And I'm not worried about the present. I'm just playing around with my future. It's all a big game. Everything we do, don't you see?"

"A big game, huh? Winner take all, victims be damned, huh? Well, I don't want to live like that."

"But you are." Millard picked up his glass, gazed at the transparent liquid between his fingers. The surface was steady, motionless.

"What's happened between us, Mac?"

"Our games got so damned serious we forgot they were games," Millard answered.

"You're one to talk about serious. When I get to feeling depressed, I jog around the park. If I'm a little tense, I play an hour or so of racquetball. That's a game. I know what a game is. But you. You run off to sea and kill yourself, while you're telling me I'm too serious? That was your latest brainstorm, wasn't it?"

"Not exactly. I'm planning to survive my death, with your help."

"It's the most harebrained scheme I've ever heard, Mac. Why should I?"

"Because you're my best friend, aren't you, James? And because I'm not as good as you are at racquetball. And because you often speak about the virtues of uncontrolled adventure, even though you never allow yourself to actually have any. And because, dear James, if you become involved in my demise, there is much less chance that you will explain anything at all to Judith when you console her over her tragic loss."

"Thorough, as usual. And over the top, also as usual."

"Thank you, James."

"Don't thank me. Just tell me why. What's the point?"

"Because. Because I'm forty-two, James. And in a few years, if I continue drifting along with the schedule that my days and weeks seem to have taken up on their own, I will be exactly nothing more and nothing less than I will be one morning when I stare at myself in the mirror and recite in just a few words exactly what and who I am. I can almost do that now; it may be too late."

"Too late for what, Mac? Why don't you take up a hobby, or a mistress? You can always expand."

"No, I can't, I'm a desperate man. Millard is dying and something else is being born. I want to see what it is."

"Try therapy, Mac. You need it."

"Therapy is so . . . secular. We dead people are into a more spiritual sort of experience. Born again, as they say." Millard grinned.

"I don't think that's what they . . . Jesus, when you get like this you're impossible. Look, I don't know whether you're right or wrong. But I'm convinced that you've talked yourself into this beyond any reasoning from me."

"That's probably true, James."

"Well, send me a postcard from the frontier when you get there. You can sign it, 'The Lone Ranger.'"

"I will, if you'll help me."

James stared at him a long moment. Millard tried to emulate the face of the panhandler: Just a buck for some food, he thought, and raised his eyebrows.

"I'll meet you on the dock, and God help me," James said.

The *Escapade* was less than a hundred yards off the stern of the *Judith-M*, and closing rapidly. Millard would not have noticed if the line from his pole had not crossed in front of her. There was a silver flash in the water off the stern, and Millard held his breath. It was a Chinook, and she would weigh maybe as much as forty pounds! He steadied the pole in his crotch and grabbed for the mike.

"*Escapade, Escapade,* stay clear of me, over." Millard dropped the mike on the deck as the star-drag sang out anew, nearly ripping out his groin.

"Mac, you listen. Now's the time! The horizon is clear, the Guard is south. Now let's get this over with. Do you read?"

"*Escapade,* stay clear. I've hooked the biggest damn Chinook I've ever seen. Do you read me?"

James's voice came faint, muffled over the radio. It sounded to Millard like "Goddamn asshole." Then James said clearly, "I'm coming alongside."

Millard steadied the mike between his cheek and collar-bone and shouted, "South Jetty, South Jetty, *Escapade.* I think we have a whole new ball game here!" He laughed, realizing the mike could not possibly be keyed on, and speculated with amusement how James would like this new game.

His pole suddenly bent double as the line veered beneath the stern of the boat. "She's a crafty witch," Millard said to himself. "She's trying to cut my line on the keel." He slacked off the tension until the pole was nearly straight. The line angled sharply beneath the boat, and Millard leaned out over the stern and stabbed the tip of his pole as deep as he could into the water. From where he was awkwardly balanced, the gold lettering that read *Judith* stared him in the face upside down.

"Oh, you're a crafty one, you are, fish," Millard said aloud. "Maybe you've been married to a hook before, ay? You divorcees are always the best scuffle." Millard saw a splash forward on the starboard side just as a ray of sunlight caught the rainbow crescent of scales, and disappeared. "So, you're after the screw with the line, are you? We'll see who gets screwed!" Millard circled the stern to the starboard side and jumped up onto the gunwale, one hand on the cabin top, and one hand holding the pole down into the water. The line angled toward the bow, and then shifted to the port side. Millard sang. "Way, hey, and up she rises. Way, hey, and up she rises. . . . Circle, my pretty! Do your worst. I've got you where I want you. I've got your whole future in my hand!" Millard swung past the bow pulpit and down the port side, hand over hand, like a spider monkey. A voice came over the radio: "Mac, I can see you on deck. What the hell are you doing out there? The time is now, or never!" Millard took his eyes off the line briefly to view the *Escapade*, idling one swell crest away. "Keep calm, Matey," he said quietly. "I can only deal with one screw at a time. . . ."

Millard had dreamt of flying, feather light, responsive to the slightest updraft, banking with just a turn of the wrist, as though playing with the wind out the window of a high speed auto. But below were the dips and slopes of the Portland foothills, the confluence of the Willamette River with the Columbia—shredded ribbons of silver. He banked to the right and soared high over the Cascades, the ski mountain a lump of melting parfait. And then to the left, out past the jagged shore of the Pacific, above the noise of the surf, into the clouds. He arched his back and broke through the stratocumulus like a jet, when the alarm clock rang. It caught him like buckshot, and he was naked, the magic of his fingers, gone. Between asleep and awake, he dropped into the sound of the bell, blinded by the rushing air, down through the panic of thick, cold clouds . . .

He thought about it as he shaved, dressed for the trip to the coast. The best dreams were those that were interrupted, as though the body knew, could sense impending change. He examined the transition of his face from Millard to someone else in the hall mirror as he passed. In the silence, he could hear Judith turn in her sleep. The mirrored figure did not turn its eyes to the sound. He searched the image for some sign of the past—scars, wrinkles, frowns, special cant of the front teeth. Perhaps some hidden glow of love or hate yet unacknowledged, for Judith, for James, for Joy, for the panhandler on the street. There was nothing apparent to him but his breath, which left a circle of fog in the middle of the face. He laughed silently. That to you, Millard. Time to fill in the blanks.

He pulled the car-keys from his jeans and checked his duffel bag. Just a fishing trip. No lucky stones from the shore of Crater Lake, no favorite bone knife bartered from a hunter in the Wallawas, no Chinese flute from the market in Victoria. All old adventures, dreams fallen out of the sky. Just a change of clothes, a new driver's license, and a bit of money. Ten grand in hundred dollar bills. Good-bye, Judith. Good-bye, house. Good-bye, moles in the front lawn. You may all assume you have won some point of contention. He closed the door without a sound.

Millard's arms ached from the pull on his pole, and beads of sweat rolled into his eyes. From the diameter of the wet line on his reel, he calculated there was still thirty to forty feet of line out. But there were fewer and fewer heavy arcs in the tip of the pole. Then the line went slack, and the pole sprang out straight. Millard cursed under his breath. He picked up the mike from where it had fallen. His hand was stiff from gripping the reel handle; it even hurt to press the mike button. "James, are you still there? I think I've lost her. North Jetty, North Jetty, over."

The *Escapade's* motor revved from the next wave trough, and when she appeared again, the bow was veering toward the *Judith-M.* Millard turned his wrist to check his watch just as the pole was jerked from his hand. The reel hung up in a cleat as it slid over the stern; Millard leaped, and caught the pole by the butt as it freed itself with a violent arc. He began reeling in again. "Way, hey, fish! You are a crafty bitch! You had me fooled. It was a nasty trick, fish. I think I loved it." Millard could see the dim flash of silver a few yards off the stern when a voice hailed him from somewhere forward.

"What the hell is holding you up now, Mac?" It was James aboard the *Escapade,* coming alongside.

"Tie up to my bow, come aboard and help me net this beauty," Millard shouted. James came to the stern of his boat and stared at him. Millard took a few turns on the reel, and grinned.

James shook his head. "Mac, you're the biggest asshole I've ever met. There's not a woman in the world worth this much trouble."

"Maybe not, James. But she's a forty-pounder if she's an ounce. You don't see them like that any more. It's the catch of a lifetime!"

"It's too late for your games now. The Coast Guard is about a half mile south and coming this way. Net it yourself. I'm leaving." James gunned the motor, and the *Escapade* pulled away.

The fish surfaced, and Millard netted it with one hand, then clubbed it to death with the gas can. He rested, breathing hard for a moment before lifting the weight into the cockpit.

Millard picked up the mike from the floor again. "James, you should see her. She's a real beauty," he said, patting the bloody head in the net. He waited, but there was no answer. He tried again. "*Judith-M* to *Escapade*. Can I borrow your hand pump? My bilge pump is electric, you know." He waited again; no response. "James, think of it as a continuing adventure. We'll maybe do it all again next weekend. Depends on the fishing."

A sound came over the radio, full of the static of distance. "Negative, you fucking asshole," it said.

"Yes we will, James, or I'll mention your name in a nasty divorce hearing. *Judith-M* over and out." Millard chuckled to himself. The sun came out from behind the nimbus clouds as they began turning white and dissipating into shards of blue. He placed a cigarette in his mouth, then remembered the gasoline. He put the matches into his pocket and the cigarette behind his ear; then he went forward to search for something to bail with, humming, "Way, hey, what a beautiful day; Way, hey; Way, hey."

THE SONG STEALERS

A LONG DAY, hunched up against the shortest night of the year, he thought. Damn long and empty. Most of the spring run nearly past. Not so many Chinook. Mostly Silvers now. Maybe I get lucky today. Maybe I catch nothing at all, get pissed off and scuttle the old scow. Head for California where everybody runs naked in the sun, like on the TV.

A motor started, then another; a rumble of creatures under the edge of a membrane. *A capella* of diesel inboards, gas generators, occasionally a jeep, or an old pickup. Awareness of the sound started in his temples, settling in his brain as upon a drum, disturbing memory: a stone in the mirror of the sea.

She said I was a fish. Takes one to catch one, she said. Fine thing for a man's woman to say. But she wasn't his anymore. She had gone over to *him*. But why did she take the money she got and buy him gifts? The little television? The Coleman stove? Out of place inside the stark, dinky cabin of the *Sea Owl*. And air freshener? Who wants a boat that smells like a forest? She was a trawler, not a damn Holiday Inn. What did the woman want? Living with another man, using his money to buy her husband gifts? Maybe she felt bad about it. "Not a fisherman's wife," she said. "Not a Quilliute, then," he had replied. "Who gives a shit about being a damned Indian?" she had answered.

But he was. Like most of the others. Maybe full-blood, maybe not. Some of the men were Umatillas, or Chilcoot. A few had some white blood, but never spoke of it. Smoke rising into the wind. The old songs were sung only by old women, and none of them knew all the words. Who knew anything but the smell of fish?

He leaned up off the wood plank bunk and stretched; his back was stiff with pain. How come when I lie down, getting up is so slow? Got to warm up careful, cough myself awake. Used to stretch every which way for fun, walked on my toes, barefoot, like a cat. Didn't give a damn for night or day. Suddenly I got hip boots and life jackets and fire-extinguishers and walkie-talkies and one-a-day pills and goddamn insurance, and a body that don't bend at all without bitching. Wrinkles as bad as the others, probably. What happened to in-between? Nothing. Still there lookin at me, like a fish-eye in a sandwich; pain is the center of all sailings, and don't you forget it. Long as you got that pain, old buddy. . . .

He rotated his shoulders until the tightness receded, then moved the Coleman from the top of his old wood stove to the bunk. He picked up a notebook and a handful of mimeographed papers, glanced at them a moment, then lit the corner of one sheet with a match. It burned slow, blue.

Government paper. You can always tell. Good for nothing; large, covered with long words and small blank places. Not absorbent. Slows people's lives up. And burns worse than

The Song Stealers

old *Newsweeks*. Don't squeeze the toilet paper, the TV said. He wadded it up still burning and lit the wood in the old stove. Can't burn government paper with a Coleman, he thought. He looked at his hands. His thumb was darkened by the burning paper. It should have stung, but it didn't. Look at those. My callouses made her skin red, she said. They don't do much for my hands, either. Maybe should use Dove. Or quit running fish leader through my palms. Maybe use my teeth, ay? Like dental floss. Then I have callouses on my face. Then people will run away and hide when I get to California to go naked in the sun. Maybe too late. My hands dead to my elbows, face like a hunting boot. Maybe it's time to learn the songs of the old women. "I'd like to sing the world a song, and tell it jokes and stuff . . ." He looked at the hands of a fisherman, tried to remember the right rhyme, gave it up. "And pull its pants down to its knees, and hump it in the buff. . . ."

He searched around for something to eat, found an open box of Winchell's doughnuts, settled back on top of the Coleman stove, and gazed out the window port. The grey was torn with strips of light; a good sign. The breeze quickened from the north and west. Also good. He would warm up the cabin with the stove while he started the *Sea Owl's* old gas heart. When it ran warm he would cast off. Maybe make it all the way up to the Umatilla Reef. Yes. A long trip, maybe a good catch of Silvers. Nothing more for a man. Except maybe doughnuts, and an Olympia beer. "Oly: it's the water." Yes, it's always the water. And running naked in the California sun. . . .

Out in the cockpit, the breeze filled his nostrils with salt and oil as his boat's engine joined the sound of the others. An old one-lunger, black from neglect, speckled with fish scales. Thirty-two feet of cedar planking, brass screws and green corroded deck fittings. On a calm day with the wind astern, she would make ten knots. Except with a wind it was never calm; he counted on six. A man could pole a dugout six knots, or paddle a canoe six knots. His short chanties need not be drowned out by the popping of cylinders. What were the songs the old women sang, which hid nothing? But a canoe had no running lights, no bilge pump, no anchor, extinguishers, depth sounders, no dugout on the cabin-top for a life boat, no outrigger poles. The *Sea Owl* carried 20 tons of gear he wouldn't need if it didn't weigh 20 tons. And was noisy. But it was his fish catcher, a Chinook killer, despite its stark low lines and lack of cabin space. It was as good as any of the trawlers at La Push, yet . . . "What getseth a man," he chanted, "to catch a damn Chinook if he loseth his god-damned soul?" Got to stop watching Easter re-runs, he thought. Plugs me up.

One early spring day before the peak of the season he had taken her with him. They had churned into an unusually glassy sea. Just a short leisurely cruise to the schools that always hung over the long reefs to the north; she could fix a lunch for them, he had said. The swells had been less than three feet; he had been able to see the small cumulus clouds mirrored in the water, suspended in stillness, except for their wake. Halfway to the reef she had retched in convulsions over the stern, then stumbled into the cabin and closed the hatch. He had squatted down in the shadows and shouted above the motor. "The fresh air will clear your head." "It's the smell of fish," she had answered. She had not spoken again, not upon their return, nor for another week.

Since then, he had lived on the *Sea Owl*, weathering out the frequent spring squalls, gazing upon the sun passing ever higher in the southern sky through the two small glass ports in each side of the cabin. Then the southern winter winds had shifted north, following the Japanese current to the Pacific Northwest coastline. With the summer trades came the warm currents, the dolphin, the herring, then the Chinook, largest of all salmon. He had visited their cottage at the beginning of the run to tell her the news; it had been empty for several days. Since, coasting like a gull, scolding glints of sun . . .

He sniffed at the wind, listened to the hum and slap of the outrigger leaders on the boats across the torn, canted walks. A few sport fishermen had their streamlined hulls tied alongside the dark trawlers. There was no room for them in the tiny bay of the Quilliute River, but there was also no port north or south for fifty miles. Besides, as long as he could remember, Sunset Fish Company had only kept up floats for enough trawlers to keep its reefers full. Most of the sleek fiberglass boats had learned not to stop at La Push. If they were lucky enough to spot the old burnt-out lighthouse on James Island a quarter mile off the coast, most failed to set for the steady north wind crossing the sand spit behind the island, striking them square on the beam. Sooner or later they would scrape off their new hull paint on lava rock reefs or rotting timber deadheads along the gauntlet of channel. If they were lucky enough to thread the southern lee of the island intact and then find a trawler willing to nestle them alongside for the night, mornings such as this one came as a cramp in their dreams, jarring the puffy sportsmen awake at five o'clock with the noise of generators and bilge pumps—and the sound of their bow lines being untied and cast into the water as the trawlers left for sea.

But the *Sea Owl* was immune; her low lines ducked the wind and her flat, tarred hull ignored the sinking spars by rote. Besides. He smiled. Anybody with any fondness for their craft at all would be crazy to argue with a mad drunken Indian bearing down on them in a hunk of shit like this covered with old black tires; he always had a berth on a choice walk.

He propped his heels on the only cockpit seat, a kitchen stool bolted to the deck. He casually examined the small cruiser tied to his port side—a Tollycraft. Twenty-eight footer.

Two radio antennae, and a tiny steel clothesline; must have a TV aboard. Radio direction finder ring and a radar dish. And two homemade outrigger poles, out of place against the factory smooth fiberglass. The cabin ports were dark; he would have to wake them to cast off.

Your Tollycraft is a woman, he thought. A young woman. My boat is an old woman. Your boat says, let's all run around naked. My boat says, let's kill fish today. My TV is a young woman singing, let's all go to San Francisco and be private eyes. Your TV is an old woman sighing, let's all go north for a rest. The wind is a woman's breath, the gulls are tears in the dress of the sky. But my woman is an ocean squall. We cast off to stroke a mad woman all day, and return in the evening to sink and drown. Why return at all, if all we have is what we take with us? But you are clever. You have a Cadillac in San Francisco, or maybe a big fine house in Portland. You can sleep late and not drown. Son of a bitch. Maybe I'll not go today at all either. Go to Hollywood instead. Be another Anthony Quinn. Maybe one more day, then *blooey.* Smoked salmon boat. Give me a reason not to coast into death through the wordless songs of those old hags. . . .

The doughnuts were gone. He washed his hands with a few lazy arcs over the stern, then took up a megaphone shaped air horn which he blew three times at the window ports of the Tollycraft. The fiberglass jolted from side to side indicating some form of life within, so he cast off both lines and backed out into the channel.

Each piling lifted its dark face like a friend; a little rudder, short drift, then back. In his youth he had scraped nearly all of them. The sportsmen still did. Maybe they were all children. Or stuntmen. A sound like an angry cat; an obscenity. A man in pajama bottoms gripped the stern-rail of the Tollycraft with white knuckles. A head behind him; pajama tops.

A voice off the port side, from the company dock. Couldn't quite hear. It was Gregor, the Sunset Company wharfinger. A black thought to ram the dock passed.

"Fill out the papers, George," the man shouted.

"Go jump in your fish bin," he shouted back.

"Fill out the forms like they said or I won't take your fish!" Gregor shouted.

He didn't answer, thought instead of his forward cabin nicely warmed by the burning papers in the wood stove. He decided he'd just beat Gregor around a little when he returned—just until Gregor took the fish. And for fun. The wharfinger's voice faded astern with shouts of something like "Coast Guard," and "Nail you!"

"Let them, goddamn it," he whispered. The company wharf disappeared as he hit the first bar swell in the widening of the channel behind the island. The force of the clean salt water against the bow slapped harbor smudge from the hull. "Hello, bitch," he said, and hummed a chorus of "Oly: It's the water."

Lieutenant J.G. Abel Radner held his binoculars with one hand, cigarette in the other. James Island Lighthouse. Good. "Steer zero-four-zero," he said.

Kiblonski swung the helm; the white cutter swung to starboard, looping as the swells caught the bow. A fine day, Radner thought. Too bad he had to waste it patrolling Indian villages. Especially La Push. Goddam fishermen either ignorant or playing dumb. But the Coast Guard had been saddled with the job: enforce regulations concerning the coastal survey of the salmon catch. Require all boats to document their catch; how many fish, what kind, where caught, when caught, how caught. Nobody liked it. The fishermen ignored it. Sunset Company avoided it, the Coast Guard griped about it. All fish caught in U.S. waters, the Department of the Interior had said, and then moved the international boundary out two hundred miles. Something about the Boldt court decision of a few years ago; something about cooperating with the Washington State Department of Fisheries, and about the Coast Guard being the only agency set up to patrol . . . "We must all work together to help protect the environment," a clean-scrubbed little man had told him at the dock in Grey's Harbor, then had rushed off to catch a plane back to Olympia. How the hell all that paperwork was going to protect anything, Radner wanted to know, but he was stuck with it. Maybe he should just steal the boat, papers and all, and head for Canada. She was a good vessel; forty feet, four crew. Engineer, Radioman, Quartermaster Kiblonski, Lieutenant J.G. Radner. Cruising range, 400 miles, food for a week. Canada, hell. Head up the coast for Siberia. Shack up with some Russian Eskimo girl. But he'd have to go through Alaska, and U.S. waters. Why the hell didn't Russia keep it? We could buy food along the way, pretend we had secret orders . . .

"Steady on zero-four-zero," Kiblonski said.

"Okay, very well," he answered. His cigarette was out. Maybe he should just dump the forms overboard. No loss to the environment; after all, that's what the Indians did with them. "Take her in," he said.

"Aye, sir," Kiblonski said. "Shall I land alongside as the welcome band plays, sir?"

Radner chuckled. "Don't fire 'til you see the reds of their eyes."

The cutter tied up to the Sunset Company dock. Not a bad entry this time, Radner thought. Only hit one deadhead; a gentle sideswipe, caught by the wind on the beam. Next time he'd make it clean. He stepped to the dock with a briefcase held awkwardly under one arm. The air was oily, the walk glistened wet in the sun. The smell of salmon mixed with sea salt burned his nostrils. Not too bad in the warmth—like an hors d'oeurve. A square, dark man stopped his work swabbing the dock planks and straightened up hard, hands on his back.

"Hey, Coast Guard," the man said.

"Gregor," Radner answered.

"I knew you'd be in today," Gregor said. "Nice weather. Fair wind, peak of the season. Good haul yesterday. Everything A-one. There's always a hawk in a fair wind."

"Shit, Gregor. Who do you call when you lose a boat, ay? Who do you call when you're crowded by the Russians? How come you always spit on the Guard?"

Gregor tightened his jaw. "Beware of the hawk who raises chickens. Give me a cigarette or I'll wipe my hands on your uniform."

"I'd throw you in the water, but I'd have to arrest myself for polluting the harbor," Radner answered, and gave him a smoke.

"I know why you're here. My cousin called from Grey's Harbor," Gregor said. "You gonna be a hard ass here too?"

"Got to. Orders from the Boss."

"Hey, you government man. Government by the people. How come I ain't you' boss, ay?" Gregor took a drag.

"We're like a totem pole, you and I. The boss is the face on the top. We're the faces on the bottom, with the dirt up to our eyebrows."

"You don't know shit about totems, Radner. Besides, we got no totems here. We are Quileute. We got TVs."

"We've got to talk, Gregor."

"Talk, asshole."

Radner took a sheaf of papers from his brief. "You've seen these before. The government wants to know how, when, where, what kind, and how much. One of these filled out every day by every boat that unloads here."

Gregor spat at the water, hit the bow line of the cutter. It hung thick, brown, like a cocoon. "I sometimes wrap fish in them, but it lowers the price," he said.

"Listen. If you don't have paper on the fish, pound for pound, no distributor in the Northwest will touch you," Radner said.

"Goddamned assholes, all of you."

"Not my doing. I've got my orders."

"That's what the soldiers said when they beat up Jesus."

"Well, they saved him from being a fishmonger," Radner said.

"Or a Coastie," Gregor answered.

"You're going to have to do it, Gregor." Radner finished his cigarette, threw it in the water. A thought flashed in mid arc that the black, scummy water would catch fire, but it didn't.

Gregor spat again, caught the cocoon in its dangle and carried it into the black. "I know," he said. "Just a fucking bother, is all. Most of the boats are okay. I give them the papers in the morning, or the night before, like you say. I sign them up, like you say. Most bring them back. A few even fill them out, except for the part about where they fish. The rest, I just fill out myself. You can't stop that. Everybody just makes up a few things and puts them down. All a lie. Who cares? Do you?"

"No," Radner shook his head.

"But some. Some won't do it."

"Then they'll lose their license."

"Shit. Who cares? Licenses don't catch fish. How you gonna take a license from an Indian? Couple of guy don't even have licenses."

"Who?"

"Who what? I didn't say a goddam thing."

Radner looked over the hull of the cutter. The walks were empty, gulls waddled along the planks. Only one or two boats not out. The sky was completely clear and quiet. A woman sat on the rock wall of the jetty across the harbor. She appeared to be facing his way. As he looked at her, she looked away. He remembered the last time he was in.

The Song Stealers

A trawler with the grimiest hull he had ever seen had come steaming in with tires over the side and deliberately side-swiped his cutter. "Sorry," the fisherman had yelled out, grinning. Wide black marks all along the port side. He remembered the name.

"What about the *Sea Owl?*" Radner said.

"Belongs to George Ottershead. He's one to steer clear of," Gregor said.

"Why?"

"An angry man. I think we'll all get by, even with these papers. The fisherman gripe. Sometimes I find fish heads in my laundry. But we work it out, no problem. Except for him. He'd like to follow the old ways."

"How so?"

"Some men are hard, but Ottershead is a damned Indian. He smokes the pipe, he sings the songs, sometimes carries an axe. He tried to teach his neighbor's kid to hunt. Gave her a bow and some arrows. Killed the neighbor's labrador, fine dog. Little girl cried. She was only six. That's when it started. Wife and him fought. He drank. Hit her once. 'Stay in the bedroom,' he always said."

"Hard man to live with."

"Impossible. She left him," Gregor spat; some of it stuck to his lip.

"What happened to her?"

Gregor smiled. It reminded Radner of a gash in the side of a dried barrel cactus, oozing liquid. "She's found a man with money, a business man who stays ashore." He adjusted and straightened his shirt.

Radner didn't answer. He knew Gregor was telling him all this only to draw the Guard into hard-nosing a rival. Maybe to get rid of him.

"Nobody likes him," Gregor added.

So. Power struggle. Tradition and regulation. Old stuff, Radner thought. Gregor would like a troublemaker out of his hair. Harass him, board him. Check his papers. Could be this man Ottershead didn't even have a license. Poor bastard's probably just barely making a living. Probably happy as a lark.

"Every boat," Radner said.

"Go piss in the sea," Gregor answered, and began swabbing the boards again.

"Kiblonski. Cast off!" Radner climbed aboard the stern of the cutter as it cleared the dock.

"Where to, Skipper?" Kiblonski said.

"North." Ropes hit the foredeck, already coiled.

The sun was straight overhead, his shadow in the cockpit not big enough to stand in. The swells were gentle and the breeze driven seas not quite breaking. He was shoreward of the Umatilla light ship anchored on the reef. On such a calm day he would troll in water as shallow as ten fathoms. His lines were humming the hook-song, and the bottom of the *Sea Owl's* reefer was covered already. The song had a blind chorus: hook spring-set, winch in, gaff aboard, club senseless, gut over the stern. He threw a fat Silver into the reefer and reached in after. "In with the silver, out with the gold," he said, and withdrew an Olympia stubby from beneath the carcasses. A swell caught the bow and pitched him against the helm stool. The beer had made his feet slow, but eased the ache in his shoulders. Sweat and fish scales clung to his bare chest and arms. Another line on the outriggers spring-snapped, setting the hook. He winched it in—a small shark. He slit its belly, watched it slide off. The gulls were on it less than thirty feet astern.

"Bleed, bastard. The more the better. Drive the whole fish city down there mad. Let 'em strike crazy—I'll reel in every last blood-junkie by a hook in their tails. Got to have a load worth a beating for." He finished the beer and pitched it over the side. A gull banked low, scolded. "Out with a fish,

in with a bottle. Even up. I'll be drunk enough to do it, too."
He thought of Gregor with his woman. The sawed off grease
ball. A wisp of cloud shaded the sun, then passed into
brightness. "I'll catch a whole reefer full, then lock him in
overnight. She'll like that. Maybe like the Mafia on *The Un-
touchables*, I'll take him for a ride. Blow him away—him, fish,
boat, and all. What the hell; the boat's insured for more than
it's worth." The woman's idea. Maybe she would come with
him to California. He thought of her round jugs bobbing bare
in the sun, and dug down beneath the fish carcasses. He'd
decide what he'd do when the time came.

The cutter ran smooth enough to maintain footing without a hand hold. Radner was at the helm; the wheel was on
automatic pilot. Kiblonski sat by the rail in the officer's seat,
cigarette in his mouth.

"Your draw," Kiblonski said. A deck of cards sat on the
compass card, face down on one side, face up on the other.
The ship's heading was visible between the cards, always lev-
eling itself.

"How far to the reef?" Radner asked.

"Destruction Island's off the port quarter," Kiblonski answered, glancing at the chart on the dashboard. "About ten
miles. Your draw."

Radner drew a card. "We'll buzz a few trawlers at five
knots, just clear of their lines, then head up to Neah Bay before dark."

Kiblonski chuckled. "I'll take the cover off the fifty caliber
on the foredeck," he said. "Just for effect."

"No you won't."

"Shit, Lieutenant. You know these goddam Indians have
got to be impressed or you won't make a goddam drop in
the bucket."

"No need to scare anybody. What we're after is coopera-
tion. Your draw."

"Yeah. And we're the only ones cooperating. Gin."
Kiblonski showed his cards. "You owe me . . . ninety thousand." He took the cards, shuffled, cut with one hand. His cigarette had an ash more than an inch long. He gently lifted it over the rail and flicked it. "Well, we're on the right trail," he said, peering into the wake.

"Why's that?"

"We just ran over an empty beer bottle. I wish they'd pitch a few full ones overboard."

"Full ones don't float," Radner said.

"Maybe we ought to steam over a few trolling lines, too," Kiblonski said.

"What's with you and fishermen?"

"Not fishermen. Indians. Indians, Jews, Wops, and Niggers. Only thing worse than one of them is all of them together."

"Comes with being a Polock, ay, Ski?"

"Polish, not Polock, asshole. You sure you're not Jewish?"

"What I am, is an officer. Deal."

"Just as bad. Almost." Kiblonski dealt ten cards onto the bottom of the compass.

"Time for one more hand. Double or nothing," Radner said.

A long hand; he lost.

"One hundred eighty thousand you owe me. Almost enough to buy Poland." Kiblonski grinned.

"Fifty times over," Radner said.

"Hey, fuck off."

"What?"

"Hey, fuck off, Lieutenant, sir." Kiblonski put a rubber band around the cards and pocketed them, then picked up the binoculars from the dashboard. "First boat ahead, sir."

"Read off the sterns, Ski."

A moment passed. "*The Dolly Ann*," Kiblonski said.

Radner slowed to five knots. The *Dolly Ann* passed abeam, six lines trolling. Its occupant was hunched over something in the cockpit. He looked up, saw the cutter, made no motions of recognition at all. Radner increased the throttle.

"Two more ahead," Kiblonski said. "Let's cut between them."

Radner looked ahead. "Not enough room." He took the helm off auto pilot and swung a point to port.

"*Susan Bee* and *Sea Swift*," Kiblonski said. As they passed abeam, one of the fishermen on the nearest boat shook a paper at them. Kiblonski chuckled.

"One ahead."

Radner swung to starboard to veer close enough to read. A moment later, Kiblonski said a name around a fresh cigarette.

"What was that?"

"*Sea Owl*," Kiblonski said.

Radner remembered the side swipe, the long scubbing away at the black tire marks. He swung the wheel hard to port, circling.

"What are you doing?" Kiblonski took the glasses away from his eyes to look at him.

"Go uncover the fifty caliber," Radner said.

"What?"

"This one's a hard case. We're going to buzz him."

Kiblonski showed his teeth in a circular grin around the cigarette. "All ri-ight . . . aye, sir!" He disappeared over the railing like a lynx.

He glanced up from the Silver he was gutting; against the horizon was a fast moving cutter—white except for the unmistakable red and blue slash under the flair of the bow. It was circling fast to port, heading toward the *Sea Owl*. He could just make out a man on the bow, uncovering the mounted gun. Then the cutter passed into the angle of re-flected sun, blinding him.

"Goddam Gregor, that son of a bitch," he whispered. "They're going to sink me." He let the Silver drop over the stern, knocking his stubby off the transom. He hit the throttle all the way forward on his way into the cabin. He searched around at random; the government forms were cold ashes in the belly of his stove. Gregor kissing his woman while he sank beneath the guns of the law! What would Charlie Bronson do now? He picked up his hand axe, then saw the Coleman stove. A slow smile played in the shadows; he put the axe in his belt. Of course! She probably didn't even like Gregor! He glanced out the cabin port. The cutter was five hundred yards off the stern. With his throttle open, he'd have four, maybe five minutes. Damn those drag-ging lines, but they had to be. It had to be natural looking. He unscrewed the cap from the white-gas tank of the Coleman stove, poured the contents over the bunk, the flooring, the anchor line, the wood-bin. The stove was the way, the TV was the teacher. What a woman. "Ah, you—you're the one . . . you dee-serve a break today . . ." He went to the cockpit, closed the hatchway behind him. The axe tore a small corner in the thick hatch-port; he took a match from his pocket. Behind him he could hear the engines of the cutter growing louder, and the gulls diving at his gutted Silver, rolling in the sun . . .

Radner cut the throttle full back; he had misjudged the speed of the *Sea Owl*. Had she been trolling, her lines would have sloped down in a steep arc to the water. But the *Sea Owl* was leaving a heavy white wake; she was steaming, her lines drawn taut, shallowing sixty yards astern. The cutter drifted over them, and they went slack as her screws slashed them in two.

"Atta boy, Skipper!" Kiblonski yelled from the bow. Radner cursed under his breath, hit the throttle to five knots, began to circle away to starboard. He'd pass slow abeam and apologize. Kiblonski was going to love that.

A hundred yards on the quarter, the trawler's cabin burst into smoke. A second later, a sound like a tree falling. Radner looked over his shoulder. The *Sea Owl* was listing hard to port, her bow completely obscured by a black ball of flames.

Kiblonski swung over the railing. "I didn't do it, Lieutenant, swear to God!" his voice thin, a whale-song. "I didn't shoot, you know that, sir!"

"Shut up and man the lifeline," Radner said, focusing the binoculars to his eyes. He could see a man in the water, holding onto the transom. The man's face was blackened; he was working his way hand over hand to the cabin top which was dipping to the water with each long swell. A gleam of something like the arc of a knife, once, twice. Then a large flat object rolled into the sea. The cutter was through the circle; Radner straightened the wheel and cut the throttle. As the sound of the engine muffled down below the slap of the small seas on the bow, Radner thought he could hear a voice shouting. No, singing. "Stand by the starboard side, Ski," he said.

As they passed astern of the old blackened trawler, she turned keel up, trolling lines draping her underside. A small object in the water nearby.

"He's in some kind of canoe, sir," Kiblonski said.

Sunlight caught the wet blade of the paddle. The man with the black face guided the shallow dugout toward the bow of the cutter, his mouth open wide, teeth showing like the grill of an old truck, arms sweeping in time with his voice. "Hey-ay-ay, Ay-ay-ay," he sang, gaining speed.

"What the hell?" Radner cut the throttle full back again, shifted the prop out of gear. The dugout was only yards away—the voice clear, hoarse, like a bear.

"Hey-ay-ay . . .G-Men! A fat fish and a full goddam beer! Take it all, will you?"

Radner watched the prow of the dugout slip under the bow of the cutter as she rose on the crest of a swell. He watched as the black Indian stood up with a hand-axe and slammed it down hard into the bow anchor sheave. The blade bounced off the metal; the man lost his balance and fell into the sea.

Radner motioned to Kiblonski, who hesitated until he saw both the man's arms flailing, empty, then threw the life ring with a line attached. The head bobbed up, streaked with soot, in the center of the ring. "You may be right about these damned Indians, Ski," he said.

"Hey-ay-ay," he coughed, "Ay-ay-ay," he shouted, then went limp. He suddenly felt naked. "Even stole my war song. Can't remember the words . . ." Grey ashes dripped in small ribbons from his eyes.

KILLER SWIMMING

EVERY ONCE IN A WHILE, I find that a simple misjudgement compounds itself with other small oversights, the effect of which is that I suddenly discover myself caught up in an error of enormous magnitude. Yesterday, for example.

My first mistake was to decide to squander my royalty check on a frivolous adventure. My fiction satire, *The Power of Positive Schizophrenia*, according to Laurence Tibbs, my literary agent in Seattle, was doing a brisk business. After a warmly negative review in *Newsweek*, requests for reading tours began to pour in, and the modest first edition entirely sold out. I myself only had six copies left, which I occasionally spread out in front of me so I could savor the large print proclaiming "The smash best seller by Thomas James Lockhart." That's me. Twenty years a hack writer of dismal fiction on the phalanx of new literary styles, and then I write a best seller in three months almost by accident. I had needed a rest from serious cynicism, and Helen, my latest, had told me this joke about a crazy person named Sam, who kept trying to build sandcastles that would resist the tide. I hadn't gotten the joke. I have long believed that all odds in modern life are impossible, so Sam seemed perfectly lucid to me at the time, within the context of the joke at least. That little misunderstanding led to the mental birth of my favorite literary device—Schizoid Sam, Man of Contrasts, who in turn has just produced my second check for twenty grand.

So I said to myself, T.J., you aren't getting any younger. Here it is the third year in a row you've claimed to be thirty-eight, and while you still have all your peanut butter colored hair, your sedentary butt is beginning to spread like jelly on a hot sidewalk. It's time to break out of so much grindstone dedication, take your crazy protagonist seriously and live on the edge of uncertainty for a few brief heartbeats.

I decided to charter a sailboat, and Helen and I would sail off into the British Columbia sunset. I saw myself at the helm, beer in hand, sucking on a Havana; Helen would be lolling in the stern, topless, soaking in the last rays of the day's sweet light. I would steer a steady course between shoals and sea creatures as the twilight deepened into close hung stars. That vision of Helen's bare breasts goose-pimpling in the night air nearly jarred my brain off its turntable, but the Schizoid Sam in me carried on as though ecstatic visions were as common as weather reports. He made inquiries, contacts, a down payment. As I said—certain visions are, well, misinterpreted.

I had no experience with sailboats, but that was not a problem. I bought several books on sailing, and a copy of *Chapman's Piloting, Seamanship, and Small Boat Handling.* I took sailing lessons in secret, on weekdays, when everyone I knew would be preoccupied with surviving workday stress.

My royalty checks were providing exquisite imprecision with respect to leisure time, and I savored each wasted hour; soon enough I would be through with my adventure, and it would back to the old word processor for me.

I chartered a sleek Catalina, a thirty foot sloop, for seven beautiful days; I planned to practice with the boat for a couple of days before I picked up Helen in Seattle. For an additional fee, the charter company had contracted to provide a young man who would teach me the finer arts of handling my sloop. I agreed to pick up the boat on a Saturday afternoon, and the two of us would sail constantly for two days. Then we would dock at the charter facility so the young man could disembark, and I would solo to the city pier to pick up Helen Monday afternoon. I planned to impress her right out of her tennis shoes. Since my athletic chest and shoulders had long since retired and gone south around my beltline, perhaps my nautical expertise and vibrant sense of adventure would relax her romantic guard. Helen, not yet thirty, was a career woman, a competant legal secretary, and had proven a tough lady to impress. But I was certain this adventure would do the trick, and had no reason to believe otherwise. I had planned carefully, completely; confidence was in my pocket.

Yesterday, which was Saturday, arrived ever so slowly; by afternoon I was so impatient to try out my new leather deck shoes and my Foster Grants that I arrived at the charter facility an hour early. The Catalina sat moored at the gas dock; I could see the charter master nimbly hopping along the deck, checking rigging, taking inventory on his clipboard.

There were others aboard, too. I could see three people; a lean, angular woman with her hair tied in a bandana, a short balding man whose obesity made me feel absolutely atheletic, and a strikingly tall, loose jointed boy with a haircut like a Marine recruit.

The charter master saw me approaching, and met me on the gas dock with a look of dismay. "Mr. Lockhart," he said, instead of hello. I had an immediate sensation that my adventure was approaching a point of jeopardy, and was all the more determined to improvise, if necessary. Schizoid Sam would.

"I'm sorry to report that the young man we engaged to skipper you cannot do so. The flu, I'm afraid." His clipboard was trembling. "Perhaps some other arrangement."

"Who's that?" a woman's rather unpleasantly shrill voice called out. The charter master turned toward the Catalina.

"This is Mr. Thomas Lockhart. He's a writer. He's signed up for the charter immediately following your departure." I heard him mutter something to himself that sounded like, "Which will be soon, I hope." Then in a louder voice, "These are the Schwartzes. Dolores, Ed, and, uh, Harley."

"A writer," Dolores said. "How nice. Have I heard of you? You look familiar."

"I doubt it," I answered.

"He's early," Ed said.

"We had arranged for some preliminary paper work to be completed, which has now become unnecessary," the charter master said. "Mr. Lockhart was to be piloted by my assistant for a couple of days, but the boy is sick."

"Rosie O'Donnell," Delores shouted. "That's where I seen you before! You were on the Rosie O'Donnell show a week ago. You know, I never miss that show. Isn't that right?"

I wasn't sure whether it wasn't right that she never missed the show, or whether it wasn't right that I had been a guest of Ms. O'Donnell a week before to speak about the virtues of creative inappropriate response. Lawrence Tibbs told me I had spoken well—animated, he said. I had rambled on about the central impetus of Schizoid Sam, that outrageous situations necessitate radical responses, and that schizophrenia was not an altogether unreasonable response to modern day life. And Sam was one character who seemed to find himself in bizarre, split-from-reality situations every few minutes or so. . . . But I had been so nervous, felt so foolish that whole week that I didn't remember a thing about the show.

"Guess so," I said to Dolores.

"Even bought your book," Dolores said.

The young man emerged from the cabin hatch. "Dolores, some of the big spoons are gone," he said.

"Shut up, Harley," Dolores said. "They all fell overboard," she said to the charter master. *"The Power of Positive Craziness;* imagine that!"

"Schizophrenia," I said.

"Most likely," the charter master muttered.

"How much money you make on a book like that, fella?" Big Ed asked. Before I could answer, Dolores elbowed him in the big balloon of his stomach, her arm bouncing away like a spring.

"Ouf," said Big Ed, and the sound became a resonance such as the Vedic masters utter in the exercise of centering. "Aum," Big Ed sang; I was afraid it would be dark before he found his center. But he rose heavily to his feet and grabbed Dolores by the arm that had nailed him. "I'm having a vision," he said, and dragged her backwards into the cabin.

"Sorry about the spoons, sir," Harley shrugged.

"It's not just the spoons, boy," the charter master said. "The bow pulpit is bent, the cabin top handrail is splintered, and two of the turnbuckles are stripped. And it looks like you poured sand in the window guides. How did all this happen?"

"Work hard, play hard. That's what Big Ed says," Harley shrugged again. "It's the Protestant ethic."

The charter master sighed. "Your folks aren't going to be so happy when I subtract the damages from their security deposit. Mr. Lockhart," he turned to me. "Perhaps when these, ah, gentlefolk depart, the two of us could sail out into the sound for an hour or two and I'll give you a shakedown."

Dolores and Big Ed emerged from the cabin hatch. "Eddy has an idea, a wonderful idea," Dolores screeched at the charter master. "You hired a boy to teach this here writer to sail, but he's sick, that right?"

"So?"

"Well, Big Eddy and me and Harley here been sailing this boat for a whole week. We can handle her pretty good now, and I'm sure you have other things to do. Now, if you was to forget about the spoons and them other little things, we'd be happy to teach him," she pointed at me with her little finger, "how to sail. Well, what do you say?"

The charter master looked at me and frowned. "Of course it's up to Mr. Lockhart entirely."

I could see that he was eager to be somewhere else. Maybe even anywhere else. And certainly two days of practice was better than an hour or two. I looked at the Schwartzes aboard my Catalina; Big Ed sat in the stern as before, smiling and humming and twiddling his thumbs. Dolores stood holding the boom, a toothy smile ripping apart her lower face. Harley stood against the helm wheel, alternately shrugging one shoulder then the other, like a two cylinder engine. They seemed harmless enough, and eager to help.

"This ain't our first charter, Mr. Lockwood," Dolores said. "We're old hands on a sailboat."

"It's Lockhart, ma'am; Thomas James. My friends call me T.J." I wondered whether I could stand them for two whole days; but I had promised to submit myself to uncontrolled adventure, and here was a bizarre opportunity already knocking. And a story I could laugh about with Helen. Perhaps they could even teach me to sail. "Okay by me," I shrugged.

The charter master threw up his hands. "Then it's okay with me, too, I guess." And under his breath he muttered something like "May the Gods be with you," but I was sure he was speaking to the boat.

"Thomas James, is it?" Dolores cooed, a sound like a pulley makes before you replace it. "Well, come aboard, Thomas James." It was nice of her to invite me aboard my own boat.

We motored out of the Ballard Narrows, Dolores at the helm, Harley coiling and uncoiling various lines, and Big Ed at the navigation table below, making pin-hole patterns in the chart with the point of his dividers. A few minutes out into the open water of Admiralty Inlet, Dolores killed the engine, and she and Harley hoisted the main sail. The wind caught its folds like a fist in the jaw, and the boat heeled over to starboard, green water almost to the deck.

"I think we should have pointed her into the wind, Dolores," Harley said, hanging from the mast.

"Shut up, Harley," Dolores said. "Lesson number one, Thomas James," she added through her teeth.

Harley hoisted the jib as Dolores guided the boat into the angle of the wind best for sail trim. I could see Big Ed from my seat in the stern; he had given up on the pinhole pictures and was now drawing burlesque nudes by connecting the random fathom markings on the chart. He was humming an off-key version of what sounded like "I Got You, Babe," a pop tune of my youth.

"Where we headed?" I shouted to Big Ed.

"Point No-Point," he answered.

"Where's that?"

"Up ahead a piece."

"What's there?"

"Ain't nothin' there. That's the point." He grinned, and began again with his humming. This time it was something not quite close to "Hey Jude."

The wind was steady but not stiff, the green of the water absorbing a blue translucence from the cloudless sky. The afternoon sun warmed my face as I turned toward it. I supposed I should be watching the helm, watching Harley tighten this line or that, but the slight roll of the hull, the taut sails lured me into the first relaxation I'd managed in weeks. I was sure Helen would love this salt air as much as I did at the moment. Dolores seemed competant at the wheel, and anyway it was too late to change the game plan now. The shore on both sides of the boat had receded into dark strips of browns and greens I knew were trees, but could no longer individualize. I reflected that in my run down condition I probably was not as strong a swimmer as I had been in my lean college years. Of course, all that green water would not have stopped Sam, who would just jump overboard, clothes, motorcycle boots, Navy peacoat and all, and start swimming. That was okay for Sam; it was his nature to test life's mettle through sheer lunacy. But short of schizophrenia, I was somewhat a captive of the situation. I closed my eyes and smiled; just what I had ordered.

"Wake up, Lockwood," Dolores shouted as she kicked me just above the ankle. I wasn't sure which was more unpleasant, her voice or my throbbing shin. "Time for your lesson!"

"It's Lockhart, ma'am," I said, rubbing my leg.

"It's Dolores. Don't you ma'am me," she answered. "Harley, get up there on deck and point to the things I say. OK, Lockwood. Time we learned you the parts of this here boat. Stand up, boy."

I stood up. The sudden movement, added to a slight change in the wind, sent me stumbling against the rails.

"First thing is, don't stand up unless you got ahold of something," she cackled, a sound utterly without lubrication. "Now, this side of the boat is called port, and this here side is called starboard." Harley dutifully pointed toward each railing. "That end is the bow, and this here is the stern." Again Harley pointed. "And that's the mast, and this here is the boom, and those wires holding up the mast are the stays." Harley swayed back and forth from his one-handed grip on the starboard stays, pumping his shoulders and pointing at one hand with the other hand.

"Now those ropes that pull the sails up is the halyards," Dolores said.

"I know," I muttered. Harley started to uncleat the main halyard, in oder to show it to me.

"Not now, Harley!" Dolores shouted. "And these here ropes that adjust the sail angles is called sheets," Dolores continued. Harley pointed.

Just then, Big Ed stood up into the passageway from the cabin, his frame filling the hatch like a huge cork. In his hands was a double-barreled shotgun; the muzzle swung around into my face. "And this," Big Ed growled, "mister hotshot writer, is a twelve-gauge bird gun." Harley pointed from the cabin top at the black figure eight just inches from my nose, which if it had been retractable, would have drawn completely back inside my head.

"What's going on?" Harley said.

"Shut up, Harley," Dolores said.

I put my hands up into the air as I remembered seeing in old time westerns, trying to form some sort of a sentence that would be meaningful under the circumstances. "Bu-uh," I bleated.

"I don't want ta have to shoot ya," Big Ed said.

"No," I managed above the pounding of my heart.

"But you're our prisoner now," Big Ed added.

"I don't have much money on me. But listen," I mumbled, "you can use my credit cards. Or take my car!"

"Don't want'cher money," Big Ed said.

"For God's sake, what then?"

"You're a writer, ain-cha?" Dolores' voice cracked as though she were chewing bubble gum full of air, an alarming mystery under the circumstances.

"Yes, I am," I said.

"You got lots o' money for that book of yours about crazy people, didn't ya?"

"Some small pittance."

"Pittance!" Dolores shouted. "Pittance! Listen to that boy talk! You'll do just fine. We don't want no money, Lockwood. We got a inheritance, Big Eddy an' me. Yes, sir, no more work at the mill for us. We're pretty, now. Money, shit. We don't need no money!"

"What's all this about then?" My arms were killing me.

"It's about Harley, here," Dolores said. I was able to tear my eyes away from those twin black holes long enough to glance at the boy. He was hanging from the boom like a gibbon, a thin thread of spittle lengthening from his open mouth. His face mirrored my lack of composure perfectly: life was one long unfathomable mystery.

"We got two whole days; you're gonna teach Harley to be a famous writer," Dolores said.

"A writer?"

"A famous one," Dolores siad, "Like the ones on Rosie O'Donnell. I see them on there all the time. They're all idiots." She had a point there. "But I'll bet they make sacks of money! You're gonna teach Harley to do that."

"But Dolores . . ." Harley whined.

"Harley, you shut up and get down here," Big Ed shouted. Harley swung from the boom to the starboard stay and then to the cockpit with such grace that he was seated before the boat recovered from the pitch of his movement.

"He's a good boy," Dolores said. "He's a great swimmer, and you should see him with a basketball. A whiz, he is. Listen to me. A poet already. It runs in the family. You'll see."

"Can't I lower my arms now?"

"Don't try anything funny," Big Ed shoved the muzzle even closer. As I lowered my arms, the barrels dropped to my sternum; I tried to sit perfectly still, so that the rising and falling of my chest would not constitute any sort of threat. Wetness spread around my armpits and began to tickle as it ran.

"So what we're going to do is sail up and down the sound here while'st you tell Harley here all you can about being a novelist and when he gets the hang of it, we'll let you go," Dolores said. "Easy as pie."

"But it's not so easy being a writer," I protested.

"You wanna be fish food?" Big Ed said.

"But Dolores, all you ever want me to do is play ball," Harley said.

"Listen, bean head. You can't make no money playing ball unless you go to college. And you can't go to college unless you earn some money. We ain't going to just give you a bunch o' money pretty as you please. You got to earn it."

"Protestant ethic," Big Ed chimed in.

"Anyway, I figure the quickest way to do that is to sell a dumb book like Lockwood here. Besides, it'll do you some good. You know how you are in English," Dolores said.

I glanced at Harley; he shrugged those incredibly loose jointed shoulders. "Flunked Lit my junior year," he said. I would have laughed, but my throat was too dry.

"Let me see if I've got this straight," I said. "You want me to teach Harley here to be a famous writer, and Harley flunked out of High School English class, and you want me to do it in two days, is that right?"

"That's the whole picture, Egghead," Big Ed said.

"But that's impossible!"

"Fish food, then," Big Ed raised the shotgun barrel.

"But we can give it a try," I added, trying hard to swallow again.

"Ain't nothing impossible. Says so on the back cover of your book," Dolores said, swinging the wheel slightly and bringing the Catalina closer to the wind.

"But that was a satire!" I said.

"Listen here, don't you use those big words on me, buster, or I'll have Big Eddy break your knees. You start from the beginning, hear?"

"Yes, ma'am," I said, understanding for the first time the dangerous nuances of the word satire.

"Call me Dolores," she smiled like the grill of a '49 Chevy, the wind stirring her hair like a bee swarm.

A drop of sweat from my forehead ran down into the corner of my eye; I blinked involuntarily, praying that that tiny gesture would not be interpreted wrongly and get me killed. My brain was already in high gear, filled with rapid-fire incomplete sentences. It occured to me that in all of Schizoid Sam's adventures, no one had ever pointed a twelve-gauge shotgun at him. The shock value of Sam's unorthodox responses to people had been enough to disarm even the most tenacious of them, in my book. But the reality of those twin barrels would not waiver, even when my train of thought organized itself into a non-stop string of verbs punctuated frequently by exclamation points. What would Sam do now? Concentrate on the gun. Sam might be crazy, but he was no fool. "Listen," I managed to gasp, "Do you suppose you could point your gun somewhere else? I promise I won't run."

Big Ed sat completely still with the muzzle pointed at me. Dolores reached over and placed her hand underneath the barrels.

"Come on, Eddy; lighten up," she said, and Big Ed raised the shotgun into the air.

"Okay," he said. "But I'm gonna set right here with it handy."

I breathed somewhat easier, which was to say, I could exhale occasionally. "What now?" I said.

"Start teaching," Dolores said, and turned back to the helm. The boat heeled slowly in the light breeze; we were in the middle of the channel, a couple of miles of green water off each beam. The only sound was the bubbling of our stern wake.

"Well," I said, trying to make eye contact with Harley. The boy sat on the starboard cushion, pumping his head up and down as though he had just memorized a long paragraph and only understood about the first three or four words.

"So, you want to be a writer, ay, Harley?" I said.

"No," said Harley. Dolores landed a toe just below his knee. "Um, yeah," said Harley. Then "OW!"

Just great. A wet chinned gibbon with a ten second delay switch between his brain and the outside world. "First thing is, Harley, a writer has to have something to say. You have anything you'd like to say?"

"No," said Harley.

"Uh, well, maybe we should talk about something you know about, Harley. Everybody is an expert at something."

"Really?" Harley grinned; I was afraid with his natural exuberance that he would hurt his face.

"Sure!" I said; I tried to encourage him to hold up his end of the conversation. My life seemed to depend on it. Big Ed was busying himself with the shotgun balanced on his thigh; he was repeatedly cocking and squeezing the trigger and letting the hammer fall on his thumb. "What can you do?" I said to Harley.

"I play basketball," Harley said.

"You like basketball?"

"Not much. Dolores makes me play because I'm tall."

"Harley!" Dolores yelled. Harley involuntarily ducked and pulled in his legs.

"It's true! You make me play ball, and I'm sick of it. You know what it's like to meet somebody and the first thing they say is, 'Hey, you're tall! You play basketball?' I'm sick of that."

"Well, you are tall. You're a nat-cheral," Dolores said.

"I wanted to go out for the swimming team, but she wouldn't let me," Harley said, looking at his hands.

"So you like swimming?" I said.

"Yeah, I swim," Harley said to his hands. "I'm pretty good, too."

"Let me think," I stalled for time to assimulate this new curve. That little outburst of Harley's added a few missing pieces to my picture puzzle of him. Harley might not be as dumb as he appeared at first; he was just nervous and frustrated. Perhaps there was something there to develop in writing which might help us both. Schizoid Sam cleared his throat and smiled. "Let's write about swimming," I said. "I always wanted to write a book about swimming." I was desperate.

"I practice as much as I can," Harley grinned. "I even read about swimming at the library."

"You've read books on swimming? On your own?"

"Lots of books."

"Then how come you didn't do well in English?"

"Can't write."

"Anyone who can read can write."

"Not me. Big Ed says so when he helps me on my homework. Still flunked."

"Help you, hell's bells, boy," Big Ed shouted, the shotgun still attached to his thumb. "I wrote your last three term papers all by myself."

"He wouldn't let me help," Harley whispered to me.

"Goddam school system anyways," Big Ed muttered.

A thought occured. "Tell you what, Harley. I'll do what I can to teach you how to write about swimming, and you can maybe give me a few pointers," I said. As I butterfly for shore, Sam whispered inside my brain.

"Guess so," Harley said. Dolores took another swipe at his shin with her deadly penny-loafers, but Harley was too fast for her and raised his legs out of range. "Sure," he said.

"Well," I said, "The first thing we have to do is make an outline. We'll need some paper and pencils. So," I clapped my hands in mock anticipation. Big Ed cocked the shotgun and stared at me; I froze with my hands in a position of prayer.

"Maybe we could get started," I swallowed. "Maybe in the cabin."

Easy as pie, Dolores had said. Right.

"Then git!" Big Ed let the hammer fall on his thumb again.

Harley and I went below. Harley found only one pencil, so I broke it in half, sharpening both stubs with a potato peeler. There was no loose paper, so I took two charts from the rack and turned them over onto the dinette. We sat down opposite one another, both of us fidgeting with our pencil stubs in silence.

Harley spoke first. "Gee, I'm awful sorry about all this, Mister Lockhart."

"Call me T.J., kid," I said. "You're the only one who remembers that my name isn't Lockwood."

"Well, I'm still sorry . . . T.J.," He grinned. I wasn't sure whether he was grinning because he was sorry, or because I allowed him to call me T.J. I decided to go with the latter. "Ed and Dolores are, well . . ." His face clouded over with the effort of thought.

"A writer has to use the exact word," I said.

"Strange," he answered.

"That's the one," I said. "Are your parents dangerous?"

"Well, I think we better do what they want," he whispered. "And they're not my parents. They're my aunt and uncle."

"How long you been a prisoner of war, kid?"

"My folks were killed in a crash when I was twelve," Harley said. "They left some money in a trust fund, but I think Dolores and Big Ed have spent most of it already. Like I said, they're kind of, well . . ." his face wrinkled.

"The exact thought, Harley."

"Well, you know how when a refrigerator's not working right and the little light goes out? Well, Dolores and Ed, they sort of have a couple of lights out, I think." When I nodded and laughed, Harley relaxed the muscles of his face a little and his natural grin came through. "Always been that way, as long as I can remember. And I'll be eighteen in two months," he added.

"Hope you make it."

"I'm going to join the Marines."

"Join the Navy, son. I was in the Navy. From what I remember, with your background, they'll make you a chief petty officer in six months."

"What?"

"Never mind." I had to remember to keep my sentences fairly short. "You know, kidnapping is a federal crime. You can't join the Marines with a rap like that."

"Navy," Harley said. His ten second delay was getting shorter. "Please, Mister Lockhart. You won't tell, will you?"

"Call me T.J., kid. And let's see how things turn out. You scratch my back and I'll scratch yours."

"What?"

"Never mind."

Harley's face slowly spread into a grin again. "Oh, I get it!" he said loudly, and laughed.

The cabin suddenly darkened; Big Ed's bulk filled the hatchway. "What's going on down there?" I could see the shotgun still locked on his thumb.

"We're just discussing the ethics of writing," I shouted, trying to smile.

Dolores struck with her penny-loafers; Big Ed grabbed for his shin with his free hand. "Leave 'em alone, Eddy. They're talking business. Besides, where's he gonna go?"

Harley leaned over the charts. "Maybe we ought to write something down," he whispered.

"Good plan," I said. I swirled my pencil stub like an artist about to freehand the Mona Lisa. I had no idea what to write down. "We need a title for our novel," I said.

"Swimming!" Harley shouted, printing the word slowly. "—I . . .N . . .G!" he said, pronouncing every scratch of his pencil stub.

"Not catchy enough by itself. Needs a modifier."

"A what?"

I drummed my fingers. This wasn't going to be easy. I took my pencil and doodled a moment, then added a word before his title.

"Killer Swimming?" Harley asked, his mouth slack, like a torn pocket. "What kind of title is that?"

"Catchy," I said. Damned appropriate too, Sam whispered into my brain.

I was fairly certain, even in the absence of a clear course of action, that I would need Harley on my side. At least, if there were any sort of confrontation, I needed him not to be on his guardians' side. And I would use any trick, any subversion I could. The only avenue open to me at the moment, however, seemed to be to write a novel. So I would have to instigate the liberation of Harley through very subtle means. I watched him sitting across from me, chewing on his pencil and then sticking it into his ear; yes, Harley would write himself into a revolution.

As I sat in the dinky, airless cabin with Harley while Big Ed clicked his shotgun hammers, my panicked brain began to push out beyond its normal limits. I felt as though someone had sliced it in two with a knife so sharp that both halves were able to go on functioning quite painlessly, without even getting in each other's way. One side of me, the cool, logical part where T.J. Lockhart lived, contemplated Harley and his furtive attempts at creativity. He was surprisingly quick to pick up ideas cast to him, and to connect disjointed ideas into linear patterns. But he was of no use when it came to thinking up new ones. Independent thought had been completely shin-kicked out of him; against the Protestant ethic, I assumed. It made me almost angry to watch his whole body tense against the tenuous grasp of a new concept, his shoulders pumping with natural exhuberance, and to know that, at least until he freed himself from the environment he grew up in, he was doomed to an arrested development. He was not, at all, an unlikable kid; maybe I could help.

By sunset, I had successfully advocated a protagonist that fit Harley down to the color of his socks, and a fairly despicable antagonist that more than subtly resembled Big Ed. The plot was simple:

> A young man named Hal, on leave from the Navy, is sailing in his dinghy with his girlfriend Helen, when they come upon a small, uncharted islet off the coast of Florida. They decide to beach the boat and explore it. Maybe they would have an adventure, or find treasure, something they could pawn for an engagement ring. (I insisted on a heroine, but Harley couldn't think of anybody he liked). Hal and Helen climb the barren slopes of the beach and find the center of the island to be much larger than they had thought—at least a mile across. In the center of the island, among large fields of low green vegetation and old wrecked cars, they find a Spanish style house. When they knock to ask if they can use the bathroom, a

man answers the door with a gun which he
points at Hal's throat. Helen faints. Hal finds
he doesn't need to use the bathroom anymore. . . .

As the shadows of sunset darkened the cabin, the T.J.
Lockhart side of me drifted off in appreciation of the most
beautiful sunset of my life, as last sunsets are prone to be.
That's when the other half of my brain tuned in. That was
the emotional side, the outrageous, fantasy ridden, edge of
panic side of me that had created and still housed my friend,
Schizoid Sam. This other side had been busy as well. Between silent fits of indignation and bottomless rage, it had
been observing, calculating. Any knowledge might come in
handy: where had the Catalina sailed, what was her position
on the chart (conveniently located on the back of our novel),
where was Point-No-Point, how was the weather, when were
the tides, what were the currents? That hemi-brain became
like a claw grasping for handholds on a glass cliff, and curs-
ing *Chapman's Piloting, Seamanship and Small Boat Handling* for not
having a chapter on "Escaping from Pirates."

Hal is strapped into the driver's seat of a
crumpled and rusted 1956 Buick. Men beat
him with radio antennae and burn him with
Buick cigarette lighters and force him face
down into the mildewed seats and make
him recite his VISA card number at gun-
point. He learns that he is being held captive
by a rebel terrorist turned atheist tour guide
named Edwardo Grande, and his henchmen, who he calls chauffeurs. Edwardo
Grande has declared his island to be an independent nation, and enforces martial law
over yachtsmen who wander ashore. He

forces the yachtsmen to eat broccoli, the national crop, until they can't stand it anymore
and buy the old Buick for the credit limit of
their charge cards. Hal is brought bowl after
bowl of foul greens; his eyes water . . .

We anchored for the night a little more than half a mile
due south of Point-No-Point in about fifty-five feet of water,
the depth of which, even Sam had to admit, was not useful
information; anything over six-foot-one was superfluous.
After a hearty meal of old, soggy tunafish sandwiches, soft
black bananas, and Olympia Beer, Big Ed lay the shotgun
down beside him so that he could indulge himself in the
fecund air of artistic talent that pervaded the occasion of my
captivity; he took up a ukelele. After fifteen minutes of "Sil-
very Moon" and "Five-Foot-Two," I professed loudly of my
weariness, which at that point bordered on nausea. Was it
the cuisine or the entertainment? Either way, the Schwartzes
surely knew how to short circuit a mutiny.

Big Ed sat in the helmseat with the shotgun in his lap,
well beyond my reach; there was nothing for me to do but
watch the twilight deepen and let T.J. Lockhart act
nonchalant while Sam figured out what to do. T.J. Lockhart
could be amazingly charming when he needed to be. It came
with practice—autograph parties, talk shows, dinners at
Mom and Dad's house. I was docile, I was pleasant, even
witty; I was careful not to be too witty though. I simply
reacted to everything as though I were wearing a lampshade
on my head. They relaxed, they laughed, they played the
ukelele. And we all drank beer. Lots of beer. I drank just
enough to convince them I was tipsy, but Big Ed plowed into
a case of Olympia like a cancer patient uncovering a cache of
Laetrile. By dark, he could hardly move anything but his
drinking arm, which, unfortunately was also his shotgun
arm. Dolores appeared about as unsteady as Big Ed; she sat

glassy eyed, with her legs spread as though braced for bad weather. Harley didn't drink at all, but he did do one curious thing; he sneaked a couple of empty stubbies from Big Ed's pile over to where my two lonely empties sat. Harley had made it appear as though I had put away enough beer to be incapable of anything but passing out for the duration of the night. There was a little of Hal in Harley after all. And I acted my part well enough; I even went so far as to stumble down the hatchway on my way to the forward cabin. Actually, I slipped and fell, but my natural awkwardness is, once in a while, a timely asset.

I closed the door of my cabin and looked around. Confining me to the forward cabin was perhaps a mistake on the Schwartzes' part. While the forward cabin was the only completely enclosed cabin, it was also the only cabin with an overhead ventilation hatch. With a little luck, it would be unlocked, and I could climb out onto the deck. Then what?

Surely Big Ed wouldn't leave his shotgun lying around where I could find it. No, he'd probably sleep with it locked onto his thumb. And if they closed the main cabin hatchway, I couldn't get at them to waylay them with a winch handle without making an awful racket. No, reason dictated a more drastic approach to liberation; God help me, I was going to have to swim for shore, just like Hal.

> Late into the night Hal slips out of his bonds and searches for Helen. When he cannot find her, he makes his way to the beach, but the boat is missing. He can just see the lights of the Florida coastline on the horizon. He tries to build a raft, but the only vegetation on the island is broccoli and it's way too short; he'll have to swim . . .

But while T.J. Lockhart had been busy tutoring Harley, Schizoid Sam had figured the tides and currents right under his nose, working them into the plot of the novel. I had found out there was a two o'clock low tide. That meant until about midnight, the waters of Admiralty Inlet would be rushing out to sea, creating a strong current which would flow north, straight toward Point-No-Point, less than two-thirds of a mile away. All I would have to do was swim straight west for about twenty minutes, and the current would wash me up onto the shore. From there I could find a house, call the police, and the rest would be newspaper headlines.

I could see the lights over the black finger of Point-No-Point reflected in the water as I went to bed; they reminded me of Hal, and Florida, and freedom. I would wait until Big Ed and Dolores passed out in their bunks before I tried the ventilation hatch. I set my digital music alarm watch for 11:45 and placed it under my pillow. I drifted off into a sleep filled with tiny green vegetation.

> Hal is having an arguement with Sam;
> Hal wants to build a raft, and Sam wants to
> hotwire the old Buick and hunt pedestrians.
> Hal is stripping off his shirt when Sam
> jumps him. They wrestle among the short
> pungent stalks; Sam bites Hal on his neck,
> but Hal dives into the surf and holds Sam's
> face underwater . . .

I awoke, choking, my pillow in my mouth; my watch was playing Beethovan's *Ode to Joy* in my ear. It was 11:45. I was afraid I had jostled the boat, but no, it was only normal wave action. As quietly as I could, I tried the levers on the ventilation hatch; they worked. Cool night air hit my face like a wet towel as I climbed out onto the foredeck. The night sky was cloudless, only a few days from a full moon. I had even calculated that time schedule as I prepared my adventure with Helen; it upset me to think that the Schwartzes planned to spoil that romantic potential. And spoil it they would; when they saw the paltry work Harley and I had completed, they would likely keep me prisoner the entire week. And Helen, stood up on a public pier, would never speak to me again. A beautiful night for anger, a blackness filled the stars, and a few points of dim light on the horizon. I could see Point-No-Point as a black ribbon between those lights and a moon-brightened sea.

> Fortunately, Hal is not only an expert swimmer, but a smart seaman. He knows these waters and such things as tides and currents. He waits until the current is flowing most favorably toward the Florida coastline. While he sits on the sand in the darkness, he gazes at the tiny lights so far away, and thinks of Helen. Where was Edwardo Grande keeping her? Was she safe and unharmed? Did she like broccoli?

I carefully stalked to the stern of the boat. No, Big Ed had not left his shotgun for me. No use delaying; I untethered the Catalina's life-ring and slipped into the water with it. Even in mid August with pants on, the water stung me with cold. I could only swim feebly for about ten minutes, then just had to cling to the life ring and await my fate.

> Hal begins swimming. Slowly at first, so as not to cramp. Then faster, until his young and supple limbs set their own cadence. Behind him he catches glimpses of the phosphorescent turbulence of his passing. He thinks of how far he has swum and

how far he has yet to swim. He thinks of
going ashore and calling the Coast Guard.
He wonders how much it costs to rent a
guided missle cruiser. He thinks about
Helen, alone among chauffeurs. He thinks
about anger. He thinks about sharks. After
about an hour, Hal's legs begin cramping;
he floats on his back for a while until the
pain goes away. He looks straight up into
the most stars he has ever seen in his life.
He picks one, a bright one with a shimmer
to it. He wonders if that is the last star he
will ever see. He wishes on it. "No," he
wishes. And the wish fills his body with the
strength to go on.

My feet touched a sandy bottom just as I was drifting off
into a hypothermic reverie about Helen, moonlight, and a
jacuzzi filled with ice cubes. I walked ashore, onto a desolate
strip of sand, driftwood, and scrubby little pine trees—and a
numbing wind. I checked my watch, 12:30. My swim had
taken thirty-five minutes. I was alone and soaking wet on a
deserted stretch of beach with not a building in sight. The
lights I had seen as I started my swim were from beyond
this point of sand, were from the next peninsula to the
north, at least five miles away. I was standing on a long strip
of beach that lay empty as far as I could see. Now what was
I to do? I was too exhausted to move another step, and too
cold to just lie down and go to sleep.

With his last breath of energy, Hal's feet
touch bottom and he struggles up through
the breakers to the beach. He crawls over
rocks and shells, old cans, foil wrappers and

used condoms until he bumps into a sign post. KEEP OFF THE BEACH, it says.

Boy scout training, dim as it was, prevailed. I built a fire structure out of driftwood branches, sheltered from the wind by a depression in the beach litter, then lit it with my Zippo lighter. A far cry from the Havana I had planned to share with Helen, but the fire warmed me down to my toes. I sat there, nestled among the driftwood logs and thought about this absurdity; I had been forced to abandon ship on a two day shakedown cruise. That was mutiny, or at least piracy. Or maybe malignant lunacy.

I fed my little fire and poked the coals together with a stick. In the sparkling flame, my outrage brought the separate compartments of my brain into individual clarity like the last moves of a Rubik's Cube. How dare those people take my boat from me? Sam had a date. And besides, my duffel bag contained substantial sections of my next book, *The Power of Positive Multiple Personality,* to which I would have to add a couple of large chapters concerning this particular adventure; but I couldn't very well do that if the Schwartzes rifled my belongings and threw them overboard, now could I? No, the time for reasonable action had passed. It was time for acts of desperation, acts of equitably lunatic frenzy. It was time for Schizoid Sam to call general quarters. It was settled then. I would have to swim back.

What a useless mess I had made of things; I could have stayed aboard and gotten a fair night's sleep. But who could have known there was nothing at Point-No-Point but sand? None of the other peninsulas were appropriately named. Hal would have known. Hal was a hero. But Thomas James was just an overwieght hack writer with wet underwear. No won-der Helen was so unimpressed about things. Well, maybe I'd change my ways, go on a diet, take up jogging, or karate. Anything but swimming. At any rate, if I lived through all of this intact, I would inadvertantly become almost like the tough as nails protagonist I had created for Harley. Jesus, my plan had backfired. I was horrified, or rather worse; I was heroified.

I knew the tide changed at two and twilight began at five-thirty; I would wait until five o'clock, when the tide would run south its strongest, just before the dawn. I found myself tightly gripping my fire-stick, a driftwood branch with a large burl on one end; it reminded me of that long bone weapon the apes discovered in the movie 2001. The violent reverie that femur-like stick stimulated in the Schizoid Sam side of me was entirely appropriate for the way I felt. I would take it with me as a kind of morale booster—or in this case, more of an ethic remover. And I would draw on that energy to win back my ship. Or become fish food, a residue of logic reflected. I would not allow that thought; I gave Sam full reign and huddled in the thin warmth without further mentation until my watch played the *Ode to Joy* at five A.M.

The tidal current ran south faster than it had run north; it was nearer to peak current. Even so, I had a tough time staying awake in the gripping cold. I took off one of my socks and made a makeshift cap out of it; I knew from Boy Scout days that most body heat is lost from the head. Most sanity too, I thought. I knew I mustn't doze off or I would drift right on past the Catalina in the poor light. So I let Sam alternate between fantasies of rage about the Schwartzes and fantasies of a more benign sort concerning Helen's breasts. Helen did have nice breasts; I had never actually seen them, but she had a firm body. She was a skier and a dancer and a runner. Not a jogger, mind you. Nothing but overdrive for Helen. I wondered what she saw in me? Untapped potential, she said I had. A strength, a depth. A MasterCharge. Dinner at the Space Needle, clinking wine goblets over the world below. Helen elicits a wry smile from me, a coolness—a numbness, actually, beginning in my feet, especially the one with no sock. I wondered if Hal would be so smart as to make a stocking cap out of his best argyles? Or dumb enough to swim back into the clutches of Edwardo Grande? I pictured Hal stripping the wire that held together the KEEP OFF THE BEACH sign, pictured him swimming back across that wide black ocean, a piece of wire in his teeth. Hal would know what to do. Hal would listen to Sam. Hal would swim ashore, hotwire the Buick and drive it through the front door of Edwardo Grande's hacienda, power shifting from room to room and squishing chauffeurs and searching for Helen and fearing the worst—maybe she actually liked broccoli. One thing was certain, though, as I clung to my lifering with one hand and held onto my thigh bone stick with the other: I was determined that no one was going to point shotguns at me anymore, nor extort me to make an ass of myself on talk shows, nor force me to eat nasty vegetables, nor dictate my literary fantasies. I was no longer inside that insipid novel; Hal had gone back to the Navy and made Sam a drill seargent. I wondered whether Helen was Sam's type? Sam wasn't fickle though; any woman was Sam's type as long as she didn't bite or kick. Especially kick. Or wasn't cold as a fish. Cold as a sleeping bag full of ice, as a swim in the Arctic Sea . . .

The sky lightened in the east enough for me to see the Catalina less than fifty yards away. I had drifted almost straight down onto her anchor line; Hal would have been proud. T.J. was too cold to do anything but thank his luck. I worked my way around to the stern and climbed out of the water with difficulty; my legs didn't respond well to Sam's commando cries.

I knew I would have to make my play before too much time went by; I was already immobile with cold, and my brain was starting to malfunction. I couldn't remember what I had swum back for. Fortunately, Sam operated quite normally under conditions of brain malfunction; he remembered he was there to bean somebody with his femur stick. All he needed was a formal invitation.

I saw his RSVP on the dashboard. At home, most people couldn't resist answering the telephone; at sea, it was the foghorn. Drunk or sober, the thought of a collision at sea destroyed everybody's prudence. It was worth a try; I took the horn and let go a long tremendous blast over the stern, then quietly stood out of sight by the companionway.

It seemed like a long time to me, shivering uncontrollably in the morning twilight, before the hatch opened. Big Ed's bird gun was first to emerge, followed by his shiny forehead. I struck down with both hands right onto his receding hairline.

"Owmm," he said. I thought he would find his center again, but he quickly found the deck with his face instead. While Dolores began screaming, I carried the shotgun forward and threw it into the compartment with my duffel bags.

"What d'ya do that for?" Dolores screamed. Then, "Asshole! What d'ya do that for, asshole?" she repeated again, nearly caving in my shinbone with her toe. She sounded to my numbed brain like the collision alarm of a Navy ship. I tried to shush her, putting a finger to my lips, but she wouldn't shush.

"You hit my Eddy, you big monster asshole!" The alarm went off again, louder and higher than before. I didn't know what to do, but collision alarms are impossible to ignore, as I said. So I let Sam bean her right on top of her hair-bun. I hated the Navy. At least it was quiet afterward.

Harley didn't say much; he just stood by the galley in his wrinkled nightshirt, pillow creases across his face like a roadmap, a strand of spittle reaching all the way over one shoulder. "Are they dead?" he said.

I looked at the two of them; Dolores lying across Big Ed like a back-pack full of sand. There was a pool of blood growing on the deck by her head. Not much of a pool, only a couple of drops, but enough to shock T.J. Lockhart back into dominance. As I looked over my handiwork, I shook my head and decided that fantasy was just too dangerous for amateurs.

"I don't think so, Harley. They're breathing."

"Oh," he answered. Then, "Oh God." Harley stood for a moment watching me shiver. "I knew you went away," he said. "Like in the story." Something in his eyes appeared almost urgent. "I thought I'd never see you again."

"Nah, kid. We forgot to finish our novel."

"I think I'm going to be sick," Harley said, looking at Dolores and Big Ed sprawled on the deck.

"I'm going to have to tie them up, Harley."

"Don't forget to tie her legs," he said. "She kicks."

Sam surfaced in my voice. "Wish we had a plank," I heard myself say.

"We don't have a plank. Besides, you wouldn't hurt them anymore, would you?"

"I don't know, kid. Adventure does strange things to a man."

I hesitated, unsure of what to do next. Visions of the Catalina pulling up to Helen's dock swam in my head, Dolores and Big Ed bound hand and foot and gagged, me at the helm, a shotgun in the crook of my arm and a Havana in my teeth.

"What are we going to do now?" Harley looked at me as though the boat were slowly sinking. I picked up the chart with our notes on it. We shrugged at about the same time.

"I don't know," I said. "Finish it, I guess."

After Hal freed Helen, they made hot dusty love among the garden greens. Hal was new at this, and found that he liked broccoli after all, pressed against Helen's white skin like the border of a chef salad. Hal also discovered that he liked tying people up. He surveyed the low hills, the cool of hacienda brick, the still salvagable Buick.

"Nice set-up," a schizoid voice murmured in his ear.

"What shall we do now, boss?" asked one of the more likable henchmen, an early defector still dazzled by the grillwork pattern on his chest.

Hal thought of his desparate swim, the terror of a shotgun held against his chest by Edwardo Grande, the green stains between Helen's shoulder blades. He smiled.

"Let's see how much tuna fish they can eat."

THE QUEEN OF ACROFAD

SUDDENLY ONE BALMY SPRING Tuesday evening, the six o'clock newscaster, new at her job as co-anchorperson and dinner hour blossom, found that she could not keep abreast of the constant gurgitation of the news teletype. Just as she began to reword the news of the latest Semite skirmish or the last update of the Panama negotiations, the machine would begin ticking and humming, automatically outdating her labors. She had worked under pressure just a moment too long; before anyone on the news crew quite knew what was happening, Jenny Jenkins had gone on camera, her face flushed, her eyes glazed, wisps of her blonde-gilded locks sticking to her forehead. Before millions of viewers within the eastern metropolitan megacity, she began to speak, quite involuntarily, only in acronyms, as if in a glossolaliac trance.

"GEFAN," she said, and smiled, a bead of perspiration poised in the hollow of her upper lip like a skier on a jump. She had meant to say, "Good evening, friends and neighbors," but could not.

"ITWONT," she said, and paused, listening. The news director began stamping his feet and moving a finger across his throat to the cameramen. The cameramen were passing a small, lumpy, tapered cigarette back and forth, and zooming in on Jenny's panic-stricken face.

"I got it," said Camera One. "In the world news today. Dynamite!"

"THE ARISLEDS MEYA TO DARLIMS," Jenny said. Camera One zoomed in on her closed eyes. Camera Two plugged in a remote microphone and finished the roach.

"The Arab and Israeli leaders met, ah, sometime yesterday I think in the afternoon to discuss arms limitations between the major Middle East nations," Camera Two said into the mike.

"SUBSUM, COPU US104S ITS, BONG PLATCONDIS, BUT WITSLEMONDI," Jenny said. But she was conscious enough to wonder how she was going to meet the payments on her flat near Central Park now that she was seconds from being fired. Her antiperspirant failed her.

Camera One grabbed the remote mike while Camera Two lit another strange cigarette. "Subject of the summit was, ah, curtailment of the purchase and use of U.S. built F104 fighter-bombers. It seems both government leaders, ah, plan to continue hostilities, but wish to spend less money doing so," Camera One said.

The News Director had frozen in mid finger slash. He routinely became flustered when things didn't progress exactly like clock gears, but this was different. He was unabashedly confused and intrigued as he watched the monitor. Jenny's beautiful platinum waves of hair had straightened and fallen past her ears, causing her face to appear narrow and receded.

"INWET," Jenny wavered, thinking about the laughter of her friends, "PRESCART AGTIFITITAB CONREST OF PANCAN TO REPAN."

"Easy," said Camera Two, breathing out a ball of green smoke and switching on the mike. "In Washington early today, President Carter agreed to a final timetable concerning the restoration of the U.S. Canal Zone to the Republic of Panama," he said, smiling. Jenny stared at the man behind Camera Two through the film forming under her grey-blue contacts, wondering how he formed words so effortlessly. She wanted to retire to the powder room with the worst kind of urgency.

"PRES AGRICONG TO TRANSOWN PANCANZ ONEFATH PERYR, BEGIDEP FATFIR," Jenny said stiffly.

Camera Two exhaled a lung-full of smoke, smiled and said into the mike, "The President agreed with Congress to transfer ownership of the Panama Canal Zone one fathom per year, beginning with the deepest fathoms first."

Jenny was totally unaware of her pronouncements, nor did she register the printed sheets in front of her. Something inside her burnt out cranium shifted into glide. She thought of her latest lover, a school teacher who often orated about the demise of the beauty and precision of proper language. He had the peculiar habit, when he was angry, of spitting as he spoke. Jenny was aware of mentioning NATO, SEATO, and OPEC, even though there was no current news about them, and imagined globules of spittle sliding down her cleavage.

"SKIRM IN ZAROIRHAR, AND BROFAM," she heard herself say. "MONUMENT."

Camera One giggled. "Skirmishes in Zaire, Rome, Ireland, Harlem, and within the British Royal family. More news on these and other puzzles in a moment."

The red lights on both cameras flicked off together, and the monitor projected a man with a bottle of mouthwash. Jenny let her face slump forward onto the desk. The news manager paced to the desk and rapped her on the back of the head.

"Okay," he sighed. "I give up. It's some kind of publicity stunt, isn't it? Or maybe a union wage ploy. You can tell me. I'm your friend," he said, wiping a sleeve across his bald pate. His cigarette, clamped between his clenched teeth, had gone out. "What are you doing, Jenny, dear?"

"DONK," she sobbed.

"She doesn't know," Camera Two said.

"You're fired. Get off the set," the manager said. "Get the backup news face in here. Fifteen seconds to go."

Jenny stood up and wiped the hair from her eyes, then began automatically to walk to the door. The cameramen whistled and clapped. "How 'bout a date in an hour?" Camera Two said.

"GO FLAK," Jenny answered, and walked out the stage exit.

"Beautiful. Perfect," Camera One said. "You can go fly a kite, Arnold."

Jenny stumbled down the Broadway sidewalk, wondering how many of her friends had seen her fall apart on the air, and now would laugh unmercifully at her for at least a year. Maybe no one had watched the news tonight. Maybe everyone was getting ready for dinner, or a date, or a dance at the Disco—but it was Tuesday. Everybody in the world stayed home and watched the news on Tuesday. Maybe she could apply for a job as a librarian in the classic literature section of the college library; not many literature majors watched the news. All she would have to do would be to walk around and say, "Shhh, no talking." She gave it a try. "SNOT," she said. Good God, maybe her affliction was permanent.

She needed a drink—a double boilermaker, and maybe a screwdriver for a chaser. Jenny thought of an object for her wandering, her favorite pub, the White Horse Inn. She paused outside, recalling how she had always preferred a bar stool under the lights to the candlelit tables. She had always felt at ease among the bottom rungs and slow risers of the insurance and corporate circuits, had found this younger, less concerned set of bearded and moustached men much more interesting than the management types she always ended up interviewing. But that was to be no more. Maybe she should just quietly marry the first broad shouldered smile that greeted her, have his kids, stay home in Brooklyn. . . . She braced herself; they might snicker, or spit. She would try one of the dark corner tables in the back.

Before Jenny's eyes had adjusted to the dim light inside, a voice shouted, "It's her!" She let her hair fall in front of her face again, and pushed through bodies toward the rear. She avoided the eyes of the men who slapped her back and carressed her shoulders. "Aych-tee, bupers," someone said, followed by a backslap. "Gee-Tee-Ess-You," another said, grinning. Someone she couldn't see was caressing her backside. Jenny turned crimson in the candle light. "DINWIME," a dark moustache said.

"GELASH," Jenny said loudly, and bit her lip. The moustached mouth froze, and a voice behind him laughed.

"She doesn't want dinner with you. She said, 'Get lost, asshole.'" Everyone clapped and cheered. "Hey, B.T., A GLEFEV" someone shouted, and everyone crowded to the bar for their free glass.

Jenny found a table completely out of the way. A new girl appeared, carrying a little round platter.

"Ordah?" the girl said, clicking her gum in a particularly Brooklyn manner.

"A BM with a SCREW," Jenny said.

"Ya got the wrong lady," the waitress said. "I'm taking drinks."

Jenny moaned and wrote her order on a napkin. A voice in the front said, "To Jenny Jenkins, Queen of ACROFAD!" Jenny began sobbing in low, deep snuffles.

Wednesday morning, Jenny experienced the worst hangover she had known since her sorority rush at Radcliffe. She did not leave her bed until noon, and then dressed only in her shower robe and bunny slippers, the way she used to when she was sick and wanted to stay home from school. The telephone rang constantly, so she removed the receiver. But she felt as though someone was there, lying on the table, listening. So she cut the cord with a pair of scissors.

She tried to concentrate on her language, and tried several times during the afternoon to enunciate slowly as she thought, 'To be, or not to be, that is the question.' But she could only blurt out, "TB OR NT TB, BG Q." She tried to relax and flow spontaneously with her mind, thinking with a smile, 'The rain in Spain falls mainly on the plain.' But she said, "RASP FALMOP," instead. She reasoned with herself that her mind was overly concerned with making connections between various unrelated objects. Perhaps, as a newswoman, she had specialized to the point of pathology. She attempted to contemplate only one subject at a time. She ambled into the kitchen and opened a cabinet, searching for the one pronounceable item. Perhaps a single can; she opened her lips and licked them in anticipation. Campbell's soup. "CREAM OF VEGBEFPOTOMPEAMUSHTRONI," she said, staring at a can of alphabet soup. She contemplated suicide. Headlines tracked across her mind. NEWSWM LPS 15 STOR TO DTH, KILLS 3 CHLRN IN FL. AND ANCRWN MXS VALIUM AND DRANO COCKTL, RELAXES INTO 50 SQ FT PUDDLE. But she was not brave, just tired. Jenny spent the evening reading the vacation ads in *McCall's* and *Redbook*. For Baja and Death Valley.

The Queen of Acrofad

Thursday morning, Jenny decided to set the *Guiness Book* world record for the longest continuous cold shower. "G.B. WOREC," she shuddered, and turned the faucet to ice cold. She had just begun to shake uncontrollably when the doorbell rang. It was the news director.

"You've got to come back to us, Jenny dear," he said, wiping his abnormally high forehead. Jenny started to form ten or twelve words, but shut her lips tight. "Do you know how many telephone calls we've had? Favorable telephone calls? Hundreds. Listen, Jenny, love. You're a hit—a sensation! You've got a swell gimmick going. People don't want to just listen anymore. They want to unravel. It makes them feel, feel . . ."

"IN," Jenny said.

"Well, yes, to use the vernacular . . ."

"IN GO ONCAM, EVAG."

He stared for a moment, with his finger stuck to his lips. "Going, yes. On camera. In going. I'm not going, yes. Ever again, yes!" His triumph faded into fidgeting. "Jenny, dear, we all love you. I may have been a bit hasty in letting you go. The station is prepared to pay you double your former wages. Ah, temporarily, of course. I mean to say, we'll work things out. And when this fad of yours wears down, well, you can just revert back to the King's English and resume your old job, simple as that."

Jenny turned red, like an apple ripening in the sun. "NOT GIM! MY MTH DSNT WK!" She started to cry, almost dropped her towel. "IM SK," she sobbed.

"Jenny, Jenny—we want you. We need you. We love you. We'll pay you triple. Just the way you are. This is a great opportunity. Do you want to starve? Think of all the fan mail. Dozens of letters already from love smitten males. Think of the joy and the liveliness you'll bring to the inner city. Not a sickness, a gift. Come back to us."

She paused, uncertain.

"Be at the studio by five," he said. "And do something with your hair."

"MB," she muttered.

"No maybe. Be there. You're the queen of ACROFAD."

"GELASH," she said.

Jenny listened to the news director as she sat next to him, just off camera. The makeup lady applied a last touch of talc to her nose and cheeks, which had already started to glow.

"A new feature of the six o'clock news," the manager said, "Newswoman supreme Jenny Jenkins will present the news in a new, ah, linguistic style which seems to be sweeping our fair city." His voice was blithe, chummy. The voice of a beagle, Jenny thought. "During the next five minute segment," he continued, "you will hear a carefully prepared synopsis of the national scene spoken entirely in the new craze dubbed by many as ACROFAD. Folks, pay attention, now; there will be a test to follow." He turned to Jenny with the kind of smile people use when they inspected their teeth in a mirror for popcorn husks. Jenny felt a hot, sick wave begin in her cowlick and sweep down over her like old coffee. She smiled back through clenched teeth, and said, "FU."

Words swirled on the news sheet before her like black bird seed. She could not focus on any one single speck. Her brain, revving, asserted a need of its own to take in everything all at once. She would have to guess what the news might be. Fortunately, she was in the habit of reading *Newsweek* and the *Midnight Tattler* on her days off.

"S.N.FEV" Jenny said, salt stinging her left eye closed. "SWEPCOUNT. MILS OF YOM . . ." She could listen to herself no longer. She shut both eyes and concentrated on the vibration in her voicebox. "Aummm," it said to her, and she blacked out.

She could hear Camera One and Camera Two alternately click on the remote microphone. She listened to them speak as though they were coaching her, straining to catch some clue that would help her concentrate on her voice. "*Saturday Night Fever* is sweeping the world of fashion," she heard the voice say. It sounded familiar, personal; but she couldn't place it. "Millions of young men are showing off their bodies in the same three piece white suits and dark silk shirts mimicking the movie idol, John Travolta. No one is allowed inside the Broadway Street Discos wearing dark clothes." Cameras One and Two clicked like a man eating pistachios. Jenny let go of her consciousness again, remembering her first venture into the tunnel of disco dancing. A young jock wearing a tanktop which said Cherry Picker's Union on the front had asked her to dance. She hadn't known how to move her feet, so she simply mimicked the others, throwing her arms, pushing out her chest and hips in slow alterations, and smiling while she thought of her favorite Boston cream pie. 'Goddamn you're hot,' the jock had mumbled.

Jenny thought of Boston cream pie. She smiled and said, "PENT DEV SON OF NUKE." The pistachios sounded again, and a voice drifted to her. "The pentagon has developed a successor to the infamous neutron bomb." Jenny thought of her lover, her teacher and mentor, who she remembered had spit on her without mercy in her last restless dreams, and who had also not called her once since this nightmare had begun. She couldn't bear the thought of his abandonment; it was as though her disease had torn a gaping hole in her being. She knew without a doubt that she was on the way to becoming a hermit. Or hermitess. Actually, she sighed, it probably didn't matter for hermits.

The voice continued outside her head: "The bomb, called a Simplex bomb, is similar to the neutron bomb in that it doesn't harm structures. But unlike the neutron bomb, the Simplex bomb does not kill people either. Instead, it leaves them with an incapacitating pubic itch. . . ."

Jenny became conscious of something cold pressing down on her forehead. It was an icebag. She was lying in a dark alcove behind the cameras. The news manager sat in the circle of blue lights, finishing his pitch, saying, "And remember, the first caller to correctly identify the last three news items will win a new cassette tape recorder like the one you see here . . ." He held up a low priced model in front of the camera alongside the sponsor's sign. The monitor lights flicked out.

So it was over. Jenny did not feel like waiting for the news director to confront her. He would either tell her she was fired again, or he would ask her to go on the air again. Either alternative made her tired. She left by the rear door without motioning to anyone.

Jenny walked along Broadway, breathing slowly, trying not to read the neon signs blinking at the dusky sky. The evening breeze arose, and small bits of paper spiralled at her feet. A car horn interrupted her stride, and she gazed around her. In the windows were diamonds, leather bags, mannikins wearing translucent chemises, microwaves, shoes—each product more desirable than the last. She thought of her late ambition, along with her carreer, to maintain a fashionable apartment, to appear in public dressed in custom tailored blouses, to order from Zales. Now her life was so torn from her desires that she was confused, lost. She had no one to turn to for comfort, and no place to hide from her nonstop brain.

The sign across the street at which she had been staring read wait; she had been content with that. But it shifted to walk, so Jenny walked. Everywhere the neon signs and placards in the windows seemed to ridicule her, as though she were walking along a parade route that bystanders had decorated in her dishonor. Fly Pan-Am, a sign blinked; Give to UNICEF, said another. GOP Headquarters. IT&T, PUD, BIG MAC. Jenny stared at the six foot plexiglass hamburger. Ten billion sold. She thought about that. It wasn't just her; she was apparently the forerunner of a giant national ideopathic disorder. And people at the newsroom thought it was cute. Wait until they hopelessly tangled their entree order at the Top of the Sixes. Wait until the man in their life leaned over on a romantic midsummer evening and whispered, "OR-IDA!" Then they would all understand, Jenny thought. But it was too tough for her to wait for the slow empathy of a derelict culture—at least while sober. She turned in the direction of the White Horse Inn.

The Inn was sufficiently crowded to force patrons out onto the sidewalk for air. Several men, and one or two women, all dressed in nearly identical light colored suits stood by the entrance, smoking and holding wine glasses by the stem. "Beau eve," a square jawed beard said to one of the pant suited ladies while she squinted through her contacts. Jenny pretended not to hear. She swung the door wide and stepped in with all the confidence she imagined a regular person would muster. She was halfway to the bar when someone behind her shouted, "It's J.J.!" Hands gripped and caressed her waist and shoulders like brushes in a car wash. "Hey-hey, Gee-Tee-Ess-You," the voices said. And, "TATAMELOV," which she interpreted as, 'talk to me, lover.' She wedged herself in next to the bar and said to the tender, "SCREW." He smiled and nodded, holding up two fingers near his watch. She gritted her teeth at him, indicating that she didn't care what time he got off work, she wanted a drink. Then she turned to face her admiring assailants, reasoning that they would not be so free with their caresses on that side. But she was a celebrity, and she was decidedly mistaken.

Anonymous hands had undone almost all of her pants buttons when she slapped the last one away and retreated with her drink to the rear of the bar. "Hi, there; Gee-Tee-Ess-You," she heard like a password, echoing like a disco beat.

"Good to see you. I-I mean, Gee-Tee-Ess-You," a familiar voice greeted her as though apologizing. It was her school teacher. She gazed into his eyes—they were bloodshot from martinis. "If you can't beat 'em, and all that," he drooled. So, nothing was sacred. The last stone had toppled. "LEMME LONE," she said, and backed toward the only escape route available—a door marked EMPLOYEES ONLY.

Jenny found a stool in the dark and sat beside a pile of boxes, too exhausted to whimper.

"Hey, lady," a startled voice shouted. "You can't be in here," the voice continued, growing more haughty. "This is an official place. Authorized personnel only. Or, A.P.O., as they say." Jenny stared at him. He was young and blond-haired, and he was dressed all in white, as though living in a stock room had bleached all the color out of him. He stared at her while she scrutinized him, then he disappeared. She sank her head deep into her hands and dreamt of long, lonely beaches of fine sand, the only sound the crash of breakers, and . . . the tapping of a cane on a tile floor.

"Young lady, you are in a restricted place. You are not supposed to be here." The voice came out of a grey tweed three piece suit with all the earnestness of a tape recorded message. She looked at him through her fingers, without lifting her head. "This is not a public part of our establishment," the tweed suit continued, tapping his cane for punctuation.

"JURSTG," Jenny mumbled. Just resting for a moment.

"I'll have your name, young lady. Be straightforward, now. You are trespassing, and you are inside a clearly posted area. This is serious!" The King of Grey Tweed tapped his cane extra hard on the tile floor, indicating an exclamation point. Jenny regarded his seriousness as a kind of truth. The gentleman believed that what he had said was unassailable. And because he did, it was. All of it. She smiled for the first time in five days; she no longer believed any of it.

"I'll have your name," the man repeated.

The Queen of Acrofad

Jenny stood up, and realized the man was surprisingly short for a commanding person; standing in front of her with his hand in a vest pocket, he looked just like Napolean. She filled her lungs with the sweet pungent aroma of old cardboard, and shouted, "MY NAME IS JENNY JENKINS!" She poked him in the chest with a finger, and he deflated like a balloon. She jumped, she danced, she twirled through the forbidden door into the crowd beyond.

"I'M JENNY JENKINS, AND YOU CAN GET YOURSELF AN-OTHER GOD DAMN QUEEN!" she shouted into the ears of the first few startled drinkers.

"Gee-Tee-Ess-You, Jenny," a tipsy voice answered. It was her teacher-friend. She cleared her throat and landed a glob on the center of his polka dot tie. "Let it blend in awhile. You certainly do," Jenny smiled. She strode with wide steps to the White Horse exit, and burst into the cool, smokeless evening air. She began, in a leisurely way, foraging along the sidewalk for a daily newspaper—one which would likely have, she thought, smiling, a large selection of Help Wanted ads.

VIEWPOINT

THE DARK SPARS OF THE JETTY were barely visible against the cliffs above the harbor. Adam guided the wheel of the *Katrina* by the position of the wharfinger's white hut at the foot of the dock. The water was calm, the color of overcast, and the old wood hull pushed through it as though it were fog. On the black line between the Georgia Straits and the low clouds, he knew he would find nothing but old white boards nailed together around a few stooped and toothless fishermen. Beside the wharfinger's shack he could now see the tiny double windows of the tackle shop. It was the only shop with windows facing the straits; nobody bought there but the Americans; they wouldn't go into a shop with no windows. The other shacks were visible now. He knew them all from the backside—the dry goods store, the grocery, tavern, cafe—sitting on the bluff above the harbor spars like skulls on a fence. Now he could smell the tar of the wharf in the morning wind, mixed with the rot of fish innards picked apart on the beach. It was a fishing village like the others he had seen: just a wharf or two that reached out from Vancouver Island into the inland passage like sparse teeth of a broken comb.

The entrance spars divided and floated by the bow on either side. Only the port entrance light shown, blinking its green shadows of blind welcome. There was a space at the end of the farthest walk, amid the clustered booms of the trawlers.

A hand pushed the door of the cabin back and Grant leaned his round sweat-moist jowls out into the cockpit. Even in the dark morning grey, with his bloodshot face, he reminded Adam of a fireplug.

"What place is this, boy?"

"Salmon Pass," Adam answered.

"This is Salmon Pass? Good."

"Good or not, it's Salmon Pass," Adam said. He could feel Grant's eyes on him; they were pushed back into his head like corks in a water bottle.

"Just land the boat, boy. I swear . . ."

Adam answered by shifting into neutral. The engine raised its pitch and drowned out the voice. The lips flapped a few more times and then Grant slid back into the cabin and shut the door.

The landing was automatic. Forward, neutral, reverse, neutral. A fur cap with a ragged bill raised up from the engine pit of the boat on the far side of the walk. The face under it was brown and blank. The man watched as Adam landed, motionless, except for a spit over the stern. Adam knew the fisherman would not offer to help land him.

When the engine shut down, Grant crawled out of the cabin on his hands and knees, as though he were afraid to touch the sides of the door with the paunch underneath his suede jacket. He stood up and slapped imaginary dirt from his hands.

"I'm going to confer with someone. Wash her down while I'm gone."

"The boat isn't dirty," Adam said.

"I'm expecting to have some people come aboard later. When I say wash it down, boy, wash it down."

"Slack water in half an hour," Adam said.

"Yeah, alright. I'll be back when I get back." The man stepped to the dock, and the boat swayed up against the black tire fenders. Adam picked up a sponge and dipped into the oily water.

The face under the fur cap did not follow Grant, but fixed on Adam as he worked. Hands under the cap took up a stone and scraped it slowly, evenly, against a cluster of salmon hooks, while the eyes moved over Adam's denim pullover, his torn gum soled shoes, his wind burnt hands, crowfeet eyes. But the fisherman said nothing.

"Got a smoke?" Adam asked.

The hands scraped at the hook a half dozen more times while the eyes remained on him. A hand disappeared into a pocket in a plaid coat soiled almost black, then tossed him a pouch. He took out his own papers and rolled a cigarette. The face across the walk settled into a pallid mask, as if it were no longer fighting the wind, and the whole coat appeared, seated on the bleached gunwale.

"You land a boat good," the old man said.

"Have to," Adam said, and tossed back the pouch.

"You an American?"

"No," Adam lied.

"Thought not. How old?"

"Twenty. How old are you?"

The old man didn't answer, knowing Adam didn't give a damn. He began sponging the deck on the dockside without looking up.

"How are the fish above the pass?" Adam said.

"Cold," the man said, and turned back to his hooks.

"And hungry," he added. "They go with the currents. With the currents, the food. With the food, the anchovy. They follow the anchovy. Don't run in schools. Run in packs, like dogs."

"And Kelsey Point?"

"The Americans are there with their Chriscrafts. The fish haven't been there for days."

Adam didn't answer. "You going up to Kelsey, ay?"

"I suppose."

"He your boss?"

"Yeah."

"You'll tell him not to fish with the others, I know." Adam dipped his sponge again, and the old man almost smiled, a lengthening of the mouth with no upturn. "Why don't you just tell him you washed it down? He'll never know the difference."

Adam laughed as the old man exposed a few yellow teeth; he dropped the sponge to the deck. "Adam," he said.

"Antoya," the man answered without moving. "Tell me, why do you work for him? Is he an uncle?"

"No, " Adam looked away. There was nothing to see that might hold a mystery. The backs of the wood shacks hid nothing but wood dust and pipe ashes, crumbs from dried pastry sent from the city. And maybe an old woman. He sometimes wondered, too.

"I work for him because I need money for school," he said.

"School, ay?" Antoya moved the stone along his hooks.

"University. Vancouver," he lied.

"I used to work in the city," the old man laughed. "During the war." He wiped the stone against his coat. The black squares in the plaid spread without edge beneath the teak of his jaw.

"You left to be a fisherman?"

"I made impeller rotors for washing machines. They went by on a big belt and I slipped in the spring center. Got tired. Wasn't worth getting paid for something that didn't mean nothing. Nothing to me, or anyone else. So now, I fish."

The ripples around the north jetty had shrunk and finally disappeared. Slack water. It was early. In half an hour, ripples would begin to curl around the base of the south jetty as the current swept down toward the pass. The tidal current running to the sea. There would be no getting through the pass then; he had seen it, and he knew. The strait, as it passed the town, was almost three miles across, but less than four miles to the north, its banks rose into jagged white rock cliffs less than two hundred yards apart. There was no other way to the sea. At the peak of the tidal current, the water began gaining speed as far below the pass as the town, and became a rush of mad whirlpools and spray in the pass itself, barring even the largest freighters. Only during the short slack between tides could one steam through safely.

If Grant delayed his return, he would miss the tide, and they would have to stay the afternoon, and probably the night. Adam had no desire to pass between the granite cliffs, even during slack water, in a cloudy twilight.

"How much time for the pass?" Adam asked. The old man did not look up.

"None."

Grant was nowhere in sight; Adam frowned. "How long does it take to get through from here?"

"Depends." Antoya looked up, then spat on his stone. "If you left now, about forty minutes, no sweat. If you leave in an hour or two, in the ebb, about fifteen minutes, in pieces.

"Thanks," Adam turned to the jetty. The ripples had just begun to curl around the south spar as the water began flowing north towards the pass. Two trawlers were nearing the entrance from the direction of the pass, having come through at least half an hour before.

"Your boss know about the pass?"

"I told him once," Adam answered.

"What will you do when he wants to go out?" The old man grinned as if for the end of a song.

"Can't go now."

"You work for these kind before? I know this kind, jabbering and mouthing in the tavern about how important everything is. He'll want to go out. When you're young, you listen to his kind because they've got the dollars, and you think they know something. But after awhile, you learn they got nothing, and they're full of shit."

"I didn't ask," Adam said. The old man disappeared into the cockpit of his boat . . .

It had been an easy job, chauffeuring for Grant. He had left Seattle after his final exams and hitched a ride north across the border expecting to pick up work in the waterfront area. Maybe get a job on a freighter going to Japan. At the end of a week, he understood a little more about longshoremen's unions and freighter crews. He gave up the idea of infiltrating the bloated market with his experience as a fisherman's boy. With less than thirty dollars in his pocket, he slept in Stanley Park, on the end of the peninsula that extended into the center of the harbor. At night he could see the lights of the docks and hear the lift trucks humming about the hulls across the inlet. He could hear the longshoremen shout, and the drop of the heavy crates. Between the lights and voices, an occasional cabin cruiser would coast by, pushing the dark water into a phosphorescent vee which would lap at his feet long after the boat was gone.

In the mornings he would walk back along the harbor side of the peninsula to the Vancouver Yacht Club and eat a bowl of corn flakes in the clubhouse cafe overlooking the docks. He always checked the clubhouse bulletin board before he left. One morning as he ate, a short man wearing a new suede jacket, the kind that light rain ruins, had swung in the door of the cafe and pinned a slip of paper on the board. The man had incredibly fat jowls like a bulldog, and seemed to lift his arms with great effort. Adam had only glanced at the paper because he wondered what a man so out of place around boats might be selling.

Grant had hired Adam that same morning, informing him of nothing but what had already been written on the paper. He was to handle the boat and pilot Grant anywhere he might need to go. That was all there was to do. That, and wash down the mahogany decks and polish the brass fittings occasionally, for three-fifty a month. Adam had asked no questions.

The two of them had left the next day for Victoria, he piloting the boat, his new employer sitting in the cabin shuffling and arranging papers from a large black briefcase. In Victoria, another man had come aboard carrying a similar briefcase, and Grant had told Adam to run and get a cup of coffee. When he had returned, the other man had already left. It had been the same in Sidney, Nanaimo, and Courteney. The men came with their cases and he was told to leave. Adam had asked no questions and the man who had hired him offered no information except that his doctor had told him to take a vacation, to get away to the mountains or the sea, and relax. The only things Adam knew for certain were that the boat was registered out of San Francisco, and that Grant had advanced him a hundred in new twenty dollar bills. And that, from observing him, Grant appeared to be incapable of taking a vacation. But he could care less for the satchel full of papers Grant guarded so jealously. He liked the boat, and piloting it was easy; that was all that mattered.

No more boats entered the Salmon Pass harbor; they had idled through the entrance spars almost as a caravan, as though they were caught in each other's tackle. He had watched them steam down from the north; they had come through the narrows on the slack of the tide, almost an hour before. He settled back against the gunwale for a long afternoon.

Grant stepped heavily into the boat, pitching the dock side into the bumpers. He carried some papers in his hand, and a newspaper protruded from his suede pocket.

"Start the boat," he said, and went into the cabin.

"Where are we going, back down to Courteney?"

"Kelsey Point."

"That's on the other side of the narrows. Can't get through now."

"Got to. Let's go."

Adam squatted down to look into the cabin. Grant put the papers into the briefcase. "Mr. Grant, we can't get through now."

Grant withdrew several sheets of small print from his case and placed them beside the unfolded newspaper. "The people I had expected to meet in Salmon Pass have already left for Kelsey Point. It's imperative that we reach them as soon as possible."

"Well, we can't leave now. It would be too dangerous, Mr. Grant. Maybe if it's so important to see them in person, you could charter a seaplane."

"There's no plane left. And I'm told the road ends only a few miles north. Anyway, we've got a perfectly good boat, and that's what I hired you for, to get me where I want to go, so let's get moving."

"I can't get us through Salmon Pass. I'm not *that* good a pilot, Mr. Grant."

Grant stopped turning the pages of the classified section and looked at him. "Look, boy. You don't understand the importance of all this, do you? No, because you're too young. But these aren't just papers I have here. These are people's fortunes. More than that—their futures, their whole lives. If I fail to push myself, if I just sit back and let these opportunities

slip by, people—a lot of people—will be hurt. Or even destroyed. You still don't understand, do you? Well, I haven't
time to explain. But it's enough to say that it's people's fi-
nances that I deal with, and a kind of speculating that I do.
So remember, time is of the essence, boy. It isn't the man
that counts, but the moment. And our moment awaits us at
Kelsey Point. If we can pull this off . . ." He paused, and
seemed to be thinking of some other place. His lips parted in
a lifeless grin.

Antoya's voice carried over the lapping water: "Good fishing tomorrow!" Adam pulled his head from the cabin and
turned toward the trawler.

"How do you know?"

"Because I think like a fish thinks," He laughed. "I don't
need to be told what water is. How good the fishing depends
on you."

"What about me?"

"Good fishing tomorrow," Antoya answered and turned
his back.

"Let's go, boy!" Grant shouted up to him.

"Tide's wrong," Adam answered.

"I know. But we have to. Anyway, it can't be that bad."

"Well, I'm not taking this boat through there now."

"You damn well are," Grant crawled out of the cabin and
stood up.

"Can't."

Grant stared at him for a moment through his black-cork
eyes. "You useless son of a bitch."

"I'm sorry," Adam said. "But you'll have to wait till morning.
Then I'll take you up to Kelsey Point bright and early."

"That'll be too late," Grant shook his head. "Time, boy. Time
is the critical factor. If you're no help to me, then you can
stay here. I'll have no more need for your services. I'll take
her through myself." Grant unfolded the chart on the dashboard and moved his finger down the number studded blue.

"Let's see, the tide is with me . . . Well, hell yes, I can make it through there," he said.

"Grant . . ." Adam said.

"Either stay or come. The boat and I are leaving."

"Grant . . ."

"You can undo those lines," Grant said. He placed a thigh across the pilot seat. The motor sputtered and revved down again.

Adam carried his leather satchel onto the walk. Green-grey bubbles of exhaust curled around the stern and crawled along the logs beneath his feet.

"You're fired, boy. Untie me."

Adam gazed instead toward the shore end of the walk, the shanty backs, the mud banks with their rotting fish. Hands unlooped the lines at his feet, and Antoya stood beside him as Grant shifted forward. The stern of the boat scraped the logs, and he had to take a step for balance. He watched the *Katrina* gain speed as it passed through the harbor, out between the spars, and behind the jetty. A drop of rain hit him on the face. Another hit his hand, then there were no more.

"I don't understand his kind," Antoya said. "What kind of papers are that important?"

"Something about people's whole lives. I don't know."

"Paper," Antoya shrugged his rounded shoulders and turned back to his trawler to pull a canvas over his tackle. "It won't rain for long."

"Do you think he'll make it?" Adam asked. The *Katrina's* wake had passed the jetty and disappeared.

"Couldn't say. But it's good you didn't go."

"Can't we call the harbor patrol?"

"Isn't any. They don't give a damn about such things here." Antoya spat across the walk at a floating can like a frog striking a gnat.

"Can't we do anything?"

Antoya finished rolling a cigarette before he spoke. "We can go see if he makes it through, if you want."

The battered green pickup rattled in and out of the gravel ruts like a trout in a spawning stream as the wheels slipped in the loose grey stones. Through the scrub trees, the straits appeared and disappeared far off down the white slopes, like the matted fur of a silver squirrel. The cliff on the far side of the strait grew higher and surged closer with every glimpse. A drop of rain parted the dirt on the windshield; through the hole he could see the passing tips of trees, the cliff, and the motionless grey sky.

The gravel widened and the truck pulled off the road beside a guardrail. There were no more trees; the rocks dropped sheer from the rail to the white water below. Across the ravine grew a single tree high up near the crest; he could see the separate needles bending in the cold breeze. Below him coiled the swirling dark holes in the spray—each vortex like the round mouth of an eel in the white froth. Adam held onto the guardrail as he looked for any small wood-dark object rushing into the rapids.

"A good hour and a half into the tide," Antoya said.

"What will happen?"

Antoya didn't answer. Adam looked in the direction the other man was looking. The cork-like movement of an object far upcurrent was accompanied by high, slow flares of white spray. It was moving faster than the current, faster than the *Katrina* could possibly go. The object disappeared as the narrows bent behind a jut in the rocks. His cheeks burned in the high breeze.

The *Katrina* hit the pools at her full speed of fifteen knots above the nearly fifteen knots of the current. The boat swung sideways and went over. He closed his eyes. There was a sound above the rush of water, a sound like the felling of a large tree. Then a sound like rocks bouncing down a stone stairway. Then, only the rush of water. His hand hurt from his grip, his eyes, his teeth. A hand on his shoulder tightened, loosened.

"It's over," Antoya said. Adam opened his eyes; he could see nothing but water. And a patch of wet rock above the waterline on the opposite wall.

"I don't understand," Antoya said. "A bunch of words. Well, no matter."

Adam couldn't answer. He formed a word with his mouth, and something inside turned upside-down; a knee gave way. He sat on the damp gravel and laid his head against the rail.

"He'll be about four miles down current before the water is slow enough for the dogfish. After the sharks, the anchovies. And the salmon. Ay, that's where the salmon will be by morning. Good fishing tomorrow!"

Adam closed his eyes again. Got to get away. Wet rock wall. Anchovies feeding on paper. Hitch a ride out. He could see the drag boats up from Courteney grappling in the morning sun below the pass, surrounded by trawlers heavy with catch. Fishermen eating rye, washing their thin smiles in the sea. Books. Drop of blood in a fish eye: *flee*

ABSENT WITHOUT LEAVE

THE SALT WIND snaps at my clothing and tangles my hair; it dries the sweat out of my shirt and makes it cold against my ribs, but that's just fine. Up from the endless rumble of the engine room, away from hot grime and oil, grease, and skin like cooked lobster, the fantail breeze is God's own breath. The sun is setting off the starboard quarter. I am so tired I hold myself up with one hand on the lifeline and stare into the propwash. In my free hand I have a cold sandwich, saved for me by the cook's helper. He saved one for Saunders, too, and I think of a face still so broken he couldn't eat it if he wanted to. I bite into the sandwich and its taste is the taste of hate for the one who did this thing: Irwin. Irwin, I think, is the one man I could kill; almost anyone on board would help me, too. Only a matter of time before someone does it. I throw the rest of my sandwich to the hovering gulls.

When they brought Sandy back aboard, he was wearing only skivvies. He was barefoot and limping, but the two hard-hats didn't even so much as hold him up when he lost his balance at the gangway. Later, after the SP's had signed him over to Chief Irwin and Irwin had rushed him below, I saw Sandy in the companionway. He had a big new purple welt under his right eye, like a patch pocket with an egg in it, and he was hunched over trying to breathe while the brig jockies hustled him along.

Sandy had gone AWOL in Guam when I had been on the quarterdeck. I was glad to be there on watch instead of down in the holds loading supplies and cargo for Danang. I was only a Third Class Signalman, which didn't cut much of a swath when cargo duty came around. And anyway, on this ship, one of the Liberty class freighters painted grey and drafted into the Navy before I was born, there were only two wartime functions: everybody loaded, or everybody off-loaded. Everybody below Chief Petty Officer, that is. Irwin saw to that. Irwin was the kind of CPO that shined his boots every morning, shaved his head every Saturday and sweat big khaki crescents into his shirt yelling at the rest of us at every opportunity. He kept a list in his shirt pocket of all the "blue boys", as in, "You take one more minute gummin' your lunch and you're on the list, you blue boy faggot!" This he would scream from distances of up to a foot, into your face, his own turning red, veins popping out along his stubby neck. And if you made Irwin's list, it meant extra duty, can-celled liberty, and sweating in the bottom of the hold until your back gave out or your hands were so bloody from the boom wires you had to have a tetanus shot. The only way off the list was to get replaced by someone Irwin could hate worse than you. But when Irwin went too long between slugs of whiskey in his coffee, everyone made the list sooner or later.

When Sandy went over, I was alone on the quarterdeck. "What's up, Sandy?" I asked him. He looked at me and smiled like he had to consider the question. It wasn't easy to know whether Saunders had answered you or not. Some thought him dumb, a typical lifer. True, Saunders was a Radioman First Class with three hash marks on his dress blue sleeve. He looked kind of dumb, in a way, too—all thin and pale and crooked. With his big hooked nose he looked as if his whole body was some kind of baldheaded screwdriver. But he wasn't dumb. Just quiet. He read actual books, and when he and I played chess, he always won. He'd play this game within the game, too, to see how few pieces he could reduce himself to and still beat me. Once he did it with a king and two pawns, just sitting and thinking, and moving back and forth, waiting for me to break into panicked flight like a game bird. Then quick and careful as a hunting dog he closed his jaws over my best game.

So when I asked him where he was going and Sandy answered "Ashore," there had been every reason to suppose he had a good reason for going there. Never mind that we were officially at Condition One-Alpha, Emergency On-Load; no one was supposed to eat or sleep or even pee until all the crates had been swung from the pier into our smelly holds. But he had those three stripes and I only had the one. And besides, we were at Guam, and there was practically no place to go for anything but official business. I had the watch radio and the watch sidearm, and I just let him go.

I went straight from watch duty to the bottom of number two hold, and Irwin made me stay there until after 0100 when we loaded the last crate. Then I went to my rack without showering and without hearing any of what passes for news around here. But by morning muster, the scuttlebutt was all over the ship; Saunders was missing. Could you believe it?

Childers nudged me as we stood in formation, and started up with that Carolina drawl: "Gone A-wahl in Guam. Shee-it! Damn speck of a island with nuthin but palm trees, tin huts and shaw patrol. Wheah's he gonna go? Stupidest thang anybody ever done who wadn't a bosun. Probly make him one soon as they ketch 'im. Three-striper, too. Wah yuh s'pose he done it, Marco?"

"I don't know," I said back, and maybe I didn't.

By the time we reached Okinawa though, Sandy was a hero, the man who went AWOL on an island so small you could walk the length of it before lunch. How small was it, the deck apes would smirk at one another. So small the airplanes landing there had to stop on the second bounce. So small, everyone on the island had the same address. So small, the national sport was incest, but only at low tide. At high tide it was palm tree climbing. A couple of days of steaming and the how small and how dumb jokes didn't even need the question to bring laughter. So dumb, he probably tried to catch a train to Phoenix. So dumb, he couldn't pour piss out of a boot with directions written on the heel.

We all knew that wherever he was, Sandy had missed ship's movement deliberately, and that he'd be in deep shit when they caught him. But we understood something about it, too; we understood about the heat of the holds, and the clawing of the fishhook frays on the boom wires into our hands, and the profanity hailing down when we stopped to press a kerchief into the blood. "Aw right you fuckin' blueboy turds, hump it, hump it right now!" the voice would say as if ten crates of folding chairs and filing cabinets, this jeep and that square of quonset siding would turn the tide of the war or preserve a life, as if it made no difference whether we bled to death right there, so long as the boom motors kept on without pause, hefting this avalanche of *stuff.* We knew what it was to chafe under our pants so bad our cotton skivvies clotted into the wounds, and how sweat stung the eyes and cut them up because of the rust and iron and manila specks that ran in little rivers off our faces. We knew what it was to hate a voice so much we could taste the meat of it and imagine cooling our faces in its blood and lifting its source up onto a boom hook, and with a wave of the hand, hauling it up and out of our lives. We knew. We hated. And we hated ourselves for it, and for just wanting it to end, simply end, without justice or honor, or pride.

But Sandy didn't hate like that. He shrugged things off most of the time. He did what he was told, ate or slept, and read his Louis Lamour books, and played chess. Chief Irwin never got a rise out of him, even when he stiff-armed Sandy into his own locker, ripped down all his books and threw them overboard. "Readers are fucking blue-boy slackers," Irwin had said then. Sandy, wordless, just gestured me and my chess board up into the shade of the smokestack when the heat of the afternoon had scorched all the other decks, and we sat there alone. Never a cuss word, except, "Damn," when I took one of his pieces. And even then it came out slow, wrapped inside a pinched up smile.

But that night in Guam, when one of the cargo containers slipped its wires and broke open in the hold, and all those air conditioners spilled out into Sandy's legs nearly breaking them, Doan the Bosun said Sandy just dropped his tailing line, picked up his shirt, and walked up to the quarterdeck shaking his head, mouth tight as a winch-wire.

As the ship steamed from Guam Harbor to Chin Wan Bay, Okinawa, the rest of us thought of Sandy and made our jokes. But secretly, for those couple of days, we let ourselves imagine him cool as James Bond, drinking champagne and smoking cigars, having magically arrived in Jamaica or Madrid. "Where would you go if you were Sandy, Marco?" the deck apes would hunker up and say.

When we docked at Chin Wan, the hardhats jerked Sandy up the gangway as soon as it was lowered. There could have been no other outcome, but we were disappointed all the same. Word soon got around; the shore patrol had caught up to him a couple of hours after the ship's departure. Found him under a palm tree on a beach just down from the Base. Nude as a jaybird, they said, sitting cross-legged and eating a raw fish. They never found his uniform, any of it, and had to borrow a pair of skivvies from a fisherman. Actually, Guam is big enough that they could have found Sandy a uniform if they had wanted to. But instead they yanked him aboard naked and chained up like a mad dog, took him below and beat the crap out of him one more time. Discipline, they called it.

Irwin saw to it that both of us got Captain's Mast; Sandy for going AWOL, and me for letting him off the ship while I was on watch. The Captain took one of his stripes and gave us both a hundred hours of extra duty. That meant we were both permanent names on Irwin's list, and that son of a bitch put us to wiping up bilge oil in the engine room as we steamed full speed from Okinawa into the Tropic Zone. Eight hours a day, plus our usual watches too; less than a week gone and I don't know how I can face even one more half hour of it. And Irwin had laughed with his boozy sneer right into our faces.

Not more than an hour ago down in the engine room, between boiler wipes, while I fought for breath in the blasts of superheated air, I asked him, "Sandy, why'd you do it?"

He looked at me, wiped his face, and panted, "Well, you know how in chess, when you're down to one piece and you just move back and forth, back and forth?"

I nodded; he'd put me there enough.

"Well, it was just my turn," he shrugged and grinned. That's all he would say about it.

I breathe in the evening wind now, and feel it sweep over my forehead like a sponge bath. Ten days more. The sun has gone down; stars appear between the clouds. I watch the horizon intently because anything closer will surely make me sick. After awhile, the horizon darkens and disappears. An almost new moon brings no light, no sparks on the wrinkled sea. I believe I could stand here forever on the fantail, gazing at the night ocean. I imagine my skin turning translucent and my eyes growing solid from prolonged exposure to starlight, like a blind fish in a cave.

I can't imagine both of the ocean's far shores at once. It is so large, it goes on for years in both directions, and I'm not more than a speck of jetsam in its beak. Soon enough it will swallow us all. Or maybe I'll slide out the other end of all this, the Navy over, and I'll go where I please. College. The corner tavern, if I feel like it. And while I'm walking, I'll look up and there it will be, this sky, clean and black and full of stars.

I hear a noise up and behind me; metal on metal, and then metal on something else.

A heavy sound then, like potatoes spilling out of a bag, up near the smoke stack. I know I should mind my own business, but the sounds are coming from my duty station. Tired as I am of the ship and all the rest of it, I feel vaguely responsible for that area. Even in the dark I can find my way around up there, so I go.

Once aloft and aft of the signal deck, I can't see a thing, but I hear an odd, intermittent lowing, and that metal sound again. I move around the stack until I step on something in the dark and stumble into the life rail as a battle lantern washes my face in a red glow.

"It's okay, it's only Marco," a muffled Carolina drawl says. Could be anyone, I tell myself. But then there is a voice I'd know anywhere, even with no more to go on than a moan. The red light is switched off quickly, but not before I see that two men with chambray shirts pulled up over their faces have Irwin tied hand and foot. Irwin's face is misshapen, and dark liquid oozes from his ears and mouth. The metal sound has come from the dark oval they are tying to Irwin's neck—a seventy pound breakdown link from the ship's anchor chain.

"Help us get him up over the rail, Marco!" one of the voices whispers. I look back at their black forms in that weak new moonlight; maybe I recognize them, maybe not. I don't want to know. All I want to remember is how close the stars are when you forget your body. I want to keep remembering them that way.

"I sure enough hate his guts," I say. "But I'm not going to help you."

"Marco, he's the King Asshole!" says the voice, the one with the drawl. "Look what he done to you and Sandy!"

"I'm not going to help you, and I'm not going to help that son of a bitch neither," I say. "I don't care what you boys do, but I don't want to remember his ugly face the rest of my life. There's nothing that important." I can't think of anything else to say, so I back away before they decide to throw me over, too.

The next morning at muster, everyone is accounted for. Scuttlebutt has it that Chief Irwin isn't feeling well. Childers has seen him in the galley, quietly filling an ice bag, his face all bandaged up, just like Sandy's was. Nobody has seen him since. "Bastard looked lahk his face uz tin pounds of burnt biscuit," Childers says, exactly as though it was a brand new sight to him. Maybe it was. Serves him right, some of the men say. Nothing'll change, others say. Saunders and I don't talk about it; we just let it drop into the wake.

Sometimes we play chess behind the stack, moving back and forth, hating the war and counting our days left in it, and trying our best to forget to count them.

MANIFEST DESTINY

MAXIMILLIAN BOYD was immediately attracted to Oak Hills the very first time he cruised the elliptical Oak Hills Drive in his new Continental Mark IV. Max had always been an ambitious man, a rising corporate star of computer-like precision, a man who owned five dozen ties (due in part to the generosity of his wife on Christmas and birthdays) and who never mismatched his slacks and blazers. It had been his good fortune to succeed in business almost without effort, but that pinnacle was not altogether satisfying. He still had to return each evening to his home and his wife, who incessantly referred to him as "my little Max." As though to disprove this diminutive endearment, Max's ambition spilled into his domestic life. It became imperative to own the tallest front windows, the greenest lawn, the longest car, the lowest golf score. So, despite his wife's jibes about his stature and abilities, Max became Number One in everything he attempted. It was his ambition; it was his destiny.

That was why Max moved his family to Oak Hills at the first opportunity. Oak Hills was the newest, the poshest of recent suburban developments that sprouted along the freeway like giant multiple kidneys. Oak Hills was the neighborhood all the corporate heads had chosen. Oak Hills had the best school, the largest golf course, the most symmetrical trees. And Oak Hills had one thing more that appealed to Max; he had noted with quiet approval that Oak Hills had a Neighborhood Association. He joined it the same day he moved into his large beige split-level.

The Oak Hills Neighborhood Association boasted over fifteen hundred members, counting kids and some of the larger dogs. Until Max moved in, the neighborhood esprit-de-corps was inspired mainly by the fact that between the railroad tracks on one side and the boggy fields on the other, Oak Hills had only one roadway entrance, inadvertently subsidizing the collective visceral impression of a fortified enclave. Capitalizing on this vague solidarity, Max initiated a vote to construct a drawbridge, arguing that the bridge could be raised on Friday and Saturday nights in order to protect their isolated community from the ravages of postgame exuberance generated at the nearby high school, an institution all regarded as a living symbol of a society gone to seed. The cost of the drawbridge was prohibitive, however. So Max diverted the growing enthusiasm of the Association into an overwhelming vote to erect rows of distinctive orange and white flags along their solitary access to the *outside*, as it was called. Enthusiasm subsequently soared; within three weeks, Max was unanimously elected chairman of the Oak hills Neighborhood Association. Max smiled quietly and held up one finger, until Max's wife smiled sweetly and said above even the loudest applause, "My little Max." Max sighed, and gazed out the window at the alder trees. "Just wait," he said, but he spoke mainly to the trees.

Within a few days, the thick old alders along the entrance way were harvested, and aluminum poles implanted in their root structures, evenly spaced. Reception of these poles and their flags was so enthusiastic that the Neighborhood Association agreed to meet weekly to discuss further improvement of neighborhood order, beauty, and morale, not to mention (although be assured it was) the preservation and possible appreciation of individual property value.

More and more old alders were cut away to be replaced by young oak saplings planted in orderly fashion along the borders of the main neighborhood thoroughfare, which was elliptical. Each home owner was allotted four of these saplings, for which he was responsible. All the residents were highly moved, and eagerly sank their saplings along the fronts of their lots, and cried for more. As a consequence of this eagerness, rules were suggested, voted upon, and bylaws adopted. All lawns were to be kept less than one and one half inches high, no dandelions allowed. There were to be no cars more than six years old left to rust in the streets. Superfluities such as boats and travel trailers were to be kept cosmetically out of sight, in garages. Changing the color of one's house paint became subject to a two-thirds vote by the Association. No unsightly swings or jungle gyms; children were directed to use the facilities at the centrally located playhouse, where parlor games were provided. It was the responsibility of individual property owners to repair fences, clean sidewalks, exterminate moles and eliminate the possibility of pet droppings with a combination of obedience school and constant vigilance. Infractions of the rules, it was agreed, would result in fines of fifty dollars per violation.

Member participation was staggering, and Oak Hills metamorphosed almost overnight into an exclusive, posh young neighborhood where citizens from proximate boroughs would chauffeur their older children in ellipses to view the artfully sculpted lawns, clean uncluttered streets, and the tasteful rotation of the five permissible house colors, hoping to instill in them a yearning for such order in their lives.

By the time the oaks were a magnificent twelve feet high, the neighborhood had accomplished uniform integrity; all the enforceable bylaws possible had long been instituted. Members lived exactly as they believed everyone else should live to arrest the undeniable decay evident on the *outside*. Land value appreciated as lawn mowers hummed and older cars were towed away. Morale soared; no fines were ever assessed, and only one family moved away, in disgrace, when their eldest son chainsawed one of the oaks in front of their home to make room for a basketball court. But the vacancy was quickly filled by pilgrims eager to comply with Association rules, who even replaced the oak at their own expense; such was Oak Hills.

Enthusiasm of this magnitude strained at the confines of mere suburban maintenance; thus the Association voted to remain active, meeting weekly at Chairman Max's house for purposes of camaraderie and seminars. Child raising forums were instituted, as were bingo and vodka. The impetus that successful cohabitation instilled manifested itself in political discussions, and further, into group therapy, Bible study, and macrame. Transcendental meditation was taught free by the wife of the street patrol captain, who was a college graduate. And pottery was turned by novices under the benign guidance of the funeral director. Each Wednesday, after all residents concluded dining, at precisely 6:30 PM, the adults strolled around the ellipse to Chairman Max's large beige split-level as a ceramic gong sounded, calling the members to meeting. The ceramic gong had been made by Max's wife and had started to be a teapot; the reason it was flat was a long story and not common knowledge. But each week, when the large ceramic dish summoned a meeting, Max's wife would smile secretively. Wednesday evenings subsequently became a festive occasion. Ties were worn; cigars were lit. Wives were swapped behind the stately brick barbecue.

Still, the full measure of their initiative was not satisfied within the elliptical perimeters, behind the flags. Max and a few older trustees more and more often discussed the vague listlessness which accompanied the fulfillment of manifest destiny. There must be new territories to conquer, Max said when occasion permitted it. New complexities to challenge, new media upon which our communal aestheticism might be expressed. The second and third trustees agreed. Perhaps we could expand in some way—branch out, Max (who encouraged everyone to affectionately call him *Number One*, no matter what his wife called him) said aloud one day. Our message of beauty through order must be carried beyond the orange and white flags, he added. The second and third trustees readily agreed, yet the plan was without form.

The Wednesday immediately following his cryptic remark, Max sounded the ceramic gong and called the Association to order. His face flushed as he slowly, almost reluctantly, began to explain his thoughts; he had the embryo of a plan. It was a hopeless plan, a token long shot, he said. But he was determined to share it anyway. All sat quietly as he explained his recent listlessness and related his vague rummaging through the family attic of souvenirs and memorabilia for some sort of inspiration or sign. He related how his halfhearted efforts had uncovered an item which might be of interest to the Association. This item from his forgotten youth had resurrected a flood of memories, of dreams, the slight promise of a star-studded destiny. He was positive the membership would understand; everyone had entered the

Publisher's Clearing House Sweepstakes with that same vague subliminal excitation: just maybe. And Max was just as positive that the membership was capable of great empathy as he recounted a young boy's vague stirrings at the breakfast table as he read from the backs of cereal boxes of far off lands. All would surely understand from their own parallel backgrounds, the logic, if not the sensibility, of his adolescent motivation in acquiring the item in question. So as not to pique their curiosity beyond its attention span, he brought forth from his coat several yellowed, brittle squares of paper; each was a deed for one square foot of land on the far Northwest frontier, along the Arctic Circle. He had acquired each one for a dollar, along with two Quaker Oats box tops, some forty years before, in an ad campaign promoting the TV show, *Sergeant Preston of the Yukon*. He had the presence of mind to struggle through ten successive boxes of Quaker Oats, the memory of which was still distastefully strong. With ten box tops, you got ten deeds and a map of the Yukon Territory, he explained. He could not find the map, but he presented the membership with the ten deeds. It was a beginning, he said, perhaps an indication of the direction they could take. Several of the members stirred, others leaned forward. The wife of the street patrol captain began rubbing her thighs together. The meeting mustered no other new business; the Oak Hills High School pep song was sung a capella, and the meeting adjourned.

The following Wednesday night, a record attendance was set, and Chairman Max's testimony was discussed. Excitement mounted as four hundred fifty members crowded into Max's large beige family room, and one by one witnessed their private reverie of the previous week. Each of the men, and a surprising number of the women, related their own childhood marathons with Quaker Oats, their dreams spurring them on, bowl after soggy bowl. By tens and twenties, the yellowed, torn squares of paper mounted the top of the

Motorola like a baptismal offering until awe subdued the entire congregation.

Long after the summer darkness fell, Chairman Max and the uppermost trustees searched the ancient documents, arranging and recording; a matrix was formed, and one of the hundred eighty two maps of the Yukon Territory consulted. Just before dawn they completed the final tabulation. Adjacent deeds filled an area, minus a few small holes, approximately twenty seven feet square. A collection plate was passed. The Oak Hills High School pep song was slowly sung a capella, and everyone went home, spent.

The following Wednesday, Chairman Max magnanimously offered to donate his vacation time for the purpose of inspecting and assessing possible use of the land designated by the deeds. He explained he had already planned a trip to Anchorage on business. It would not be far out of his way to fly further north for a couple of days. In his absence, the second trustee would organize such morale boosters as name-the-new-territory contests and raffle lotteries, the winners of which to become trustees of the unnamed land. Trial charters would be drafted, rules and bylaws experimented with. The new land, small and inaccessible as it was, presented all with a tiny jewel of hope and fascination. Chairman Max was toasted several times with vodka martinis; everyone called him *Number One,* (except his wife) and enthusiasm surpassed even that of the raising of the orange and white flags.

Upon his return, Chairman Max initiated the back fence network, and a Wednesday night meeting was called, even though it was only Monday. It was reported that he had sounded grave. The gong was sounded, the meeting called to order, and the old business was perfunctorily disposed. Chairman Max rose wearily, and the members fell silent, shocked at his appearance. He had a five o'clock shadow, and his tie was askew.

He reported from the beginning, of his business meeting in Anchorage, his flight to Fairbanks, his search for a bush pilot, his supper at the Fairbanks Howard Johnson's, his flight over the uneven tundra, the melting ice floes, the pipeline. The surveyor he had employed had double and triple checked, incurring great expense; there was no mistake about the final resting place of New Oak Hills (as it was called after the contest). Chairman Max downed a vodka straight and presented the membership with the simple facts.

Their plot of land was roughly twenty seven feet wide by thirty one feet long, not considering the few hundred missing pieces; the plot lay at approximately 69 degrees, 46', 55.76" North Latitude by 101 degrees, 22', 46.852" West Longitude; the plot lay in the exact center of the concrete cap on the top of the silo of a Niki Dewline Defense Warhead; the fine for his trespassing on military security ground was five hundred dollars. His court hearing would be the following Wednesday.

There was no meeting two days later, Chairman Max having flown out the day before to prepare his case. Nor the following week, as he had not returned. But a few days thereafter, the back fence network sprang to again to life, and that evening, the Oak Hills Neighborhood Association assembled on the back patio of the second trustee's large beige split-level. He quieted the banter, and the old business was perfunctorily dismissed. The second trustee produced a letter addressed to the entire membership, which he proceeded to open. It explained how Chairman Max had presented his case to the Federal District Court in Fairbanks. His case, stated roughly, argued that since the land, approximately one-half square acre, had originally been legally purchased by Quaker Oats, which in turn had legally relinquished ownership to its numberless legion of patrons, of which the Association was the legal majority (no one else ever having had the temerity to claim their land), Chairman

Manifest Destiny

Max had indeed not been trespassing, since he was the legal owner of the property. Furthermore, as for the Governmental claim to the land in question, the Federal Government could not have legally condemned the land without proper notification of the said condemnation to its previous owners. since the Government had illegally seized the land, their claim to said property was actually null and void. The jurists decreed that since Chairman Max had the proper legal documents (all ordered and arranged), that he was indeed the legal owner of the entire half-acre of land in question. However, since the land had been under military jurisdiction and improved upon after that fashion, it could not fall under the legal dominion of any land oriented organization or interest group. Therefore, Chairman Max explained, the property on which the Niki Dewline Warhead sat had been signed over directly to him. As a result of this tremendous responsibility, and because the Federal Government owed him $400,000.00 in back lease fees and taxes, he felt it was his solemn duty to remain in litigation at Fairbanks. Meanwhile, he would busy himself learning how to operate the small black console that came with the missile. The letter included a return post office box number, and warmest regards. The meeting was silent for a moment, until someone began to hum the Oak Hills High School pep song. Everyone joined in, and the meeting adjourned.

The following Wednesday at the regular meeting in the second trustee's large beige split-level, the old business portion of the meeting deteriorated scandalously into numerous spirited speculations about the well being of Chairman Max. No one had received any word from the chairman since his original letter. But then too, it was remembered that Max's wife, who was very fond of pottery, had moved in with the funeral director, was attempting to perfect with him the furtive techniques which produced flat teapots, and had not bothered to check the mail box for several days. Chairman Max's neighbor, who had been out measuring the chairman's lawn, reported that his mail box had been empty. A motion was passed to dispatch a letter to the return post office box number instructing Chairman Max that his lawn be kept under the prescribed one and one-half inches. The High School song was played on the ocherina by the second trustee's preschool daughter (who was perhaps a prodigy) and the meeting adjourned.

A week later, after the pre-meeting vodkas, all members of the Oak Hills Neighborhood Association solemnly gathered in the second trustee's large beige family room. No one had heard from Chairman Max since his first and only letter. Old business was readily dismissed, and the second trustee began itemizing the complaints. Chairman Max's lawn was five inches high; his Buick had been stripped by vandals and lay on its side in the street like a shell. His son had broken his arm skateboarding into one of the oaks, and despite the pain, had had the temerity to cut three of them down before the ambulance arrived. His daughter had been sponsoring loud, boisterous parties which lasted until long after the supper hour, and at which laughter and fast records were heard simultaneously. It was speculated that this might be the same crowd of hoodlums which had overturned the family car. Step by step, the violations were tabulated, and a letter drafted to Fairbanks, inquiring as to the well being of Chairman Max, expressing deep concern about his reticence, and fining him nine hundred fifty dollars for violations of the Oak Hills Neighborhood Standards. He could afford it, they said. The Oak Hills High School pep song was sung a capella, and the meeting adjourned with the membership confident that the problem would surely be dealt with immediately. Chairman Max had always exhibited a precise and resolute disposition.

Two Wednesdays passed without a meeting as the heat of summer accelerated, but then the back fence network

interrupted the familiar routine to report that a sealed letter
had been found in the high grass near Chairman Max's mail
box. A meeting was called for the following Wednesday, at
the second trustee's large beige split-level. At exactly the
usual time, the ceramic gong (one of several) was sounded,
and the meeting was called to order; the old business was
perfunctorily dismissed. A sealed letter was presented to the
second trustee by Chairman Max's neighbor, who held it
aloft for all to see the Fairbanks return post office box number. The second trustee ceremoniously opened the letter and
read it aloud for all to hear; to wit:

To the Oak Hills Neighborhood Association

Dear Friends;

I have been working all day instituting the
most efficacious organization of this half-acre
of which I have grown quite fond. It is ex-
ceedingly beautiful here in the summer on
the tundra. I should like to live here. But there
is a large blight in the center of my lot which
upsets me daily with increasing disgust. This
missile shall have to be removed. Fortunately,
I am learning ever more about the complexities of the large black console which directs
the aforementioned blight, and I believe I can
now operate it without failure. The question
is, of course, where to dispatch it.

I have built a small cabin on the side of
the silo; with the missile gone, I am sure the
silo will suffice quite comfortably as a salon
against the approach of winter. I grow to
much prefer this boundless silence, this
spiralling midnight sun. And there are visitors,

too, oh yes—Eskimo women are very beautiful and friendly (and also very short).

I received your letter dated Wednesday last, and it distresses me greatly to discover how quickly loyalty is supplanted by amnesia. But perhaps my family will have occasion to reflect upon my good will toward them as we struggle to reinstitute the ties that bind people to one another. All things considered though, I cannot depart this enterprise at present, as there is much to accomplish in preparation for the long cold nights ahead. The agitation and frustration is almost too much to bear, however, when I think of my beautiful former home in such disrepair; we all ought to be ashamed.

Therefore, I implore you, do not disregard my beloved hearth; do not interrupt the integrity of the Association of which you are so proud. Take it upon yourselves to maintain my lawn and repair my house, replace my auto and my oaks, for I cannot be interrupted in my contemplation of how I will empty my salon. For the sake of practice, I have painted the nuisance orange and white, and fed it your coordinates.

Warmest Regards,
Number One

GUNNER'S MATES

Danang Harbor, 1968

THE SUNLIGHT COULD not quite penetrate the suspended swirls of dust inside the ship's hold. Shirtless, I
leaned my wet shoulders against a crate marked "Extreme
Danger—Do Not Smoke" and waited for the next descent of
the boom wires. Williams lay on top of the crate, oblivious to
the dirt settling into the puddles of sweat on his black chest.
Far above us, the deck plates formed a square of light into
which occasionally a small head would appear. Then a voice
would drift down, indistinguishable, absorbed by the pumping drone of the boom engines.

   A trampled shred of palm leaf drifted down, glancing off
my arm. A helo ripped across the white square, then a
muffled blast a long ways off. I imagined the fireball opening

like a huge, orange flower. I pushed the thought away and looked for the heavy cables coming down.

The boom wires tapped and twisted across the deck toward us, and together we stopped their swing to load another crate. My hands no longer hurt more than my back. As the load blocked the light on its way up, Williams lit a cigarette and offered me one.

"Says do not smoke, man," I said.

He looked at me and pointed a cigarette butt at his chest. "I know what's in these crates. Do you?" he said, his lips pulled into a smirk as he slid another one onto a pallet.

I nodded, but he told me anyway. I loaded the next one, and wiped my hands on my pants when I was done. The smoke from Williams' cigarette would not rise, it was so hot.

"And you know what they do with it, right?" he asked.

I looked at our blue chambray shirts cast aside on the deck. I knew that by that night after my shower, the crate on which Williams had been sitting would be open and empty, its contents strapped to the helo gunship underbellies. By morning we would be at sea again, steaming to pick up another load.

Another muffled blast, felt more than heard. Then another.

"Man, they're cookin' tonight," Williams said.

I imagine faces under straw hats lifting skyward at rotor sound. The fireball opens like a flower; it is too late to run . . . I breathed away the image.

Williams took a deep drag on his cigarette until the ash glowed, then he touched it to his forearm for an instant. His mouth moved, and his eyes, but he made no sound. "You know, they say there's no way'n hell to put it out," Williams said, grinding the cigarette butt into the deck with his heel.

"I don't want to think about it," I said. I tried to breathe deeply, but the thick dust made my throat spasm.

Gunner's Mates

"Seen it once, afterwards," Williams taunted me. "Man, that yellow skin must burn just like grease. Nothing left but bones 'n ashes." He looked down at his shoes; the laces were broken and knotted.

"I wonder what kind of skin burns best," I muttered. Maybe I said it to shut Williams up, and maybe I said it just to shock my brain into waking, far from there. I remembered reading that a hundred years ago there had been slaughters at Sand Creek and along the North Platte. The papers had called them baffles, but the warriors were all away in Canada. I see women asleep under the skins, children dropping their stick toys and staring toward the sound of hoofbeats . . . I see some bucktoothed artillery man blocking the cannon wheels and opening the ammo cases. *"But I don't see no men,"* he says. *"They're all the friggin' enemy. Open the breech,"* the Gunnery Sergeant answers.

"Young skin. Old skin," Williams shrugged. "Scared stiff shit-your-pants skin. It's always the wrong people. Some shit don't change." He looked my way as though if I were any other color, I'd know.

We were out of pallets; nothing to do but stand there until the deck crew lowered some down. I tried to slow my breathing, and closed my eyes. But I saw the old woman again. She was alone, standing on the beach as we landed our mike-boats on Batangan Peninsula. I remembered how she began shuffling toward us, bowing and offering something in her outstretched hands as we rushed out of the surf. And how her wizened face relaxed after we shot her. *"What the hell d'you do that for?"* someone had said. *"Thought it was a friggin' rifle,"* someone had answered.

"I know," I said. Again I remembered the rouged-up faces in the candle glow of the Danang bars, each one glaring behind a tight smile that whispered, *"You killed my grandmother!"* And voices from the vegetable carts, stand bars, and bicycles weaving by, chanting the only Vietnamese I knew; *'Thit khee!*

Monkey meat.' The old woman had only been selling monkey meat on a stick.

I examined my hands; they were bloodied from the fish-hook frays in the boom wires. "But what can we do?" I said.

"Have a cigarette," Williams said, and blinked a bead of sweat from his lashes.